Sheriff Wall watched Barbara walk outside, leaving the reception behind.

Ordinarily he wouldn't have followed her, but if anyone was going to make contact with her, they would do it at some event like this—a wedding—where they'd blend in. Strangers stood out in Dry Creek, but tonight any number could walk around, and no one would pay attention as long as they had a cup filled with punch.

Of course, the sheriff wasn't worried about Barbara seeking her ex-husband's criminal partners. He'd talked with her enough to know she wasn't likely to turn to crime. But that didn't mean her ex-husband's partners wouldn't try to get to him through her. Yeah, the sheriff told himself, he'd better go talk to her—just to make sure everything was okay….

Books by Janet Tronstad

Love Inspired

*An Angel for Dry Creek #81
*A Gentleman for Dry Creek #110
*A Bride for Dry Creek #138
*A Rich Man for Dry Creek #176
*A Hero for Dry Creek #228
*A Baby for Dry Creek #240
*A Dry Creek Christmas #276
*Sugar Plums for Dry Creek #329
*At Home in Dry Creek #371

*Dry Creek

JANET TRONSTAD

grew up on a small farm in central Montana. One of her favorite things to do was to visit her grandfather's bookshelves, where he had a large collection of Zane Grey novels. She's always loved a good story. Today, Janet lives in Pasadena, California, where she is a full-time writer.

Janet Tronstad

AT HOME IN
Dry Creek

Steeple
Hill®

Published by Steeple Hill Books™

STEEPLE HILL BOOKS

Steeple
Hill®

ISBN-13: 978-0-373-81285-1
ISBN-10:   0-373-81285-X

AT HOME IN DRY CREEK

Copyright © 2006 by Janet Tronstad

www.SteepleHill.com

Printed in U.S.A.

Except the Lord build the house,
they labor in vain that build it.
—*Psalms* 127:1

This book is dedicated to all of the
Mrs. Hargroves of the world who teach
Sunday school, befriend their neighbors
and do good to others.

Chapter One

It wasn't against the law for her to catch the bridal bouquet, Barbara Strong told herself as she cupped her hands to catch the flowers that had been thrown so expertly at her. Besides, if the bride didn't care that the bouquet went to someone who wouldn't fulfill the prediction of being the next to marry, what did Sheriff Wall care?

The sheriff was standing across the room from Barbara and scowling at her as if she'd just lifted the silverware. There was enough music and chatter all around that Barbara doubted anyone else noticed the sheriff's frown—especially not now that everyone was looking at *her*.

Great, she thought, as she forced herself to smile. The whole town of Dry Creek, Montana; all two hundred people, had seen her catch Lizette's bridal bouquet, and now they had one more story to tell each other about her.

For months, Barbara had thought that the interest people here showed in her and her two young children had been because their arrival was the only thing that had happened in this small town for a long time. The days had been cold and people hadn't been able to make the trip into Billings very often. Some days there had been so much snow on the roads no one went anywhere. Added to that, everyone had complained that the television reception had been worse than usual for some reason this past winter.

People had been bored.

Barbara had understood why they would be looking for something new to entertain them. But she and her children had been here almost five months now. In television terms, they were last year's reruns. Nobody should be watching them with such keen interest, especially not the sheriff.

The chatter increased as people came up to Barbara and congratulated her. It was dark outside, but inside the large community center, strings of tiny white lights glowed along the rustic wood walls. A circle of people stayed around Barbara after the initial flurry of congratulations had died down.

There was a full minute of awkward silence as everyone seemed to stare at their shoes or boots and wait for something. Now that they had her surrounded, Barbara realized, they didn't quite know what to do with her.

Charley, a white-haired man, was the first one to clear his throat.

"I don't expect you've had a chance to meet my nephew. He lives in Billings," Charley said as he stepped closer to Barbara and lowered his voice. Charley was one of the first people Barbara had met when she'd arrived in Dry Creek last fall. "I don't mind saying he's a fine man. Single and he loves kids. Works as a mechanic in a shop, too, so he could provide for a family—even now he might be able to fix you up with a car so you'd have one. Sort of a courting present, you know—like flowers. He's good with cars."

Charley and some other old men spent their days around the woodstove in the hardware store and they seemed to know more than most people about what was going on in this small town. Barbara respected Charley. He had been a rancher all his life and still had a tan line on his forehead that marked where the brim of a straw hat would normally sit. He knew about hard work. He was also one of the leaders of this community. His roots went deep here. That was one reason why Barbara wasn't as annoyed as she could have been with his matchmaking.

"You know I can't accept a—" Barbara started to say. She'd begin with the obvious protests and work her way up to all the reasons she wasn't ever going to get married again.

"Oh, it'd be his pleasure, don't worry about that. He'd love to help out a pretty young woman like yourself."

Charley smiled at her. Barbara thought he looked relieved to have his piece said.

Jacob, one of the other old men who regularly sat by the woodstove, shook his head in disgust. Jacob was the one who had invited Lizette, who had just married Barbara's cousin Judd, to come to Dry Creek and open up her dance studio.

"She's young all right!" Jacob protested. "I don't know what you're thinking. That nephew of yours has to be fifty if he's a day. If no one cares about age, I could court her myself. And I'll be seventy-six this July." Jacob's voice rose higher with each word he said and his gray beard quivered with indignation. "Come to think on it, maybe I will do just that—if you can't come up with someone better than your nephew! Besides, what's wrong with that son of yours? He's sitting out there on that ranch of his not more than five miles from here. He could use a wife—and he's young enough." Jacob looked around the room. "Where is he anyway? I don't see him here."

"He doesn't come to weddings," Linda, the young woman who owned the café, said softly as she stepped closer to Barbara's side. "Besides, Charley's son is already in love with someone else. We need to find Barbara a man who's going to be hers exclusively. That's the only way it can really work."

Barbara was surprised to smell jasmine

perfume on Linda. In the five months she had known the café owner, the young woman had seemed to go out of her way to avoid perfume and skirts and anything that would hint that she was an attractive woman. Usually, she just wore a big white chef's apron over her blue jeans and T-shirt.

Linda had spoken of some unrequited love in her life one morning when she and Barbara had sat at a table in the café and shared a pot of tea. Barbara wondered if Linda was thinking of that love now, whoever he was. If she was, it had brought a wistful, fragile look to her eyes.

"I'm sorry, but I'm not—" Barbara tried again. She looked at the faces around her. She liked all of these people. She didn't want to disappoint them. She just wished they could have asked her for something she could give. "Of course, I appreciate it. But you don't need to—"

"Don't you worry none about finding a man who will be yours altogether. My nephew will be faithful," Charley interrupted staunchly. He'd found his second wind, Barbara thought in dismay. "He may be old, but he's a fine man. Committed."

"Well, I'm committed, too, if that's all you need," Jacob replied.

"Should *be* committed is more like it, you old coot," Charley said. "No one here is talking about you."

Barbara saw the vein grow more pronounced on Charley's neck.

"No one needs to be committed," Barbara said as she held up her hands in surrender. A petal or two fell off the bouquet as she lifted it. She made sure she smiled when she talked. She supposed she should be touched that people were worried about finding her a new husband. "It's all been a mistake. I didn't mean to catch the bouquet; it was just reflexes. The thing was coming at me and I just grabbed it so it wouldn't hit me. It doesn't mean anything. I'm not looking for a husband."

She didn't add that now that she'd had a moment to think about it, she wished she'd had enough sense to duck when she'd first seen the bridal bouquet heading her way. Failing that, she should have let it hit her square on. She wasn't sure if she'd live long enough for the story of how she'd caught

Lizette's bouquet to fade from the minds of everyone around here.

That was because every story about *her* lasted longer than it should. That was what had finally made Barbara realize something was wrong.

Barbara had been okay with all of the interest at first. She'd moved around enough to know how it was when a new person moved into a small town. The heightened-interest stage came first, but usually it didn't last long, and once it was over, someone would ask the newcomer to serve coffee at a PTA meeting or head up a fund-raiser for the school, and that was an official sign that the person was no longer an outsider but a member of the community.

Barbara was prepared for this cycle. She wasn't sure how many times the person needed to pour coffee before they *really* belonged to the community, but she figured it was probably somewhere around a thousand cups of coffee poured at various functions.

It was the after-coffee place that Barbara wanted to reach—the place where she was a comfortable part of everything just as these people standing around her now were part of it all.

She'd begun to wonder if she'd ever reach that place.

There was a moment of silence as the conversation stopped swirling around Barbara. There was still noise elsewhere in the community center, but the circle around Barbara had grown quiet.

"I suppose we can't blame you for not looking for another husband—you probably still have feelings for the one you have," Charley finally said quietly.

"Of course she has feelings," Linda agreed and then sighed. "Sometimes that's just the way of it. No matter what you do, the feelings stay with you."

"They say even geese mate for life," Jacob added with a grunt. "Doesn't matter what kind of a bird they end up with, they stay hooked to that one. Reckon it's the same with her and him."

Barbara shook her head. Finally, they were at the heart of why the people of Dry Creek were so fascinated with her. If it had only been she and her children who had moved to town, the others wouldn't have been interested for so long. No, the interest was mostly because of *him*.

Her ex-husband was sitting in the jail in Billings awaiting trial for robbing several gas stations. It was obvious that the people of Dry Creek were watching to see what happened with her and Neal before they welcomed her into the fold and asked her to do something as simple as pour coffee for them at some function. Barbara wasn't sure what people expected to learn about her by waiting, but she had a sinking feeling that at least some of them were wondering if she was going to play Bonnie to her ex-husband's Clyde.

Barbara didn't know how to explain to everyone that Neal no longer held any part of her heart or her life. He didn't have the faithfulness of a tomcat, let alone a goose. She wouldn't follow him *anywhere*…and certainly not into a life of crime. If she had learned anything from Neal, it was that crime ruined lives. She'd never be Bonnie to anyone's Clyde.

She hesitated long enough that a whisper

came from somewhere behind her. Barbara knew she wasn't supposed to hear it.

"Poor thing. She's so brave," the woman's voice said, low and filled with pity. "And him sitting there in jail—he's not worth it."

"Hush, now," another woman hissed. "He must be worth something if she married him."

Barbara knew she wasn't the only one who heard the whispers because there was a sudden chorus of throat clearings and foot shuffles. She hoped no one expected her to answer the whispers. Barbara wasn't upset that people wondered about her and her ex-husband—she just didn't know what to say. She wanted these people to truly welcome her into their community, and she doubted anything she said about Neal would make that happen. If they didn't trust her to be an honest citizen, they wouldn't trust her any more because *she* said she would be one.

From the first day Barbara had driven into Dry Creek, she had wanted to belong here. She'd been frantic with worry that day because she was trying to locate her second cousin, Judd Bowman, so she could beg him to take care of her children while she drove to Denver to check out an abused woman's shelter that might take them. Bobby was six at the time, Amanda was five. Now, they were both a year older.

Even in her distress, Barbara had noticed that the town offered its residents the opportunity to put down roots. It had clotheslines that were actually being used and old men who sat around a potbellied stove in the hardware store and talked. It was obvious that people really knew each other here. When Barbara's husband was finally arrested and she was released from the hospital where his beating had put her, she was glad she could come back to a place like Dry Creek.

But becoming rooted here wasn't as easy as she had thought it would be. She and her children had been here since November, and she hadn't poured a single cup of coffee. Even now, although she was a bridesmaid at this wedding for Judd and Lizette, no one had allowed Barbara to do more than walk up the aisle.

People still treated her like a visitor, and she didn't know what to do to change it. At this rate, she wouldn't be accepted into this town until she was lying in the cemetery behind that little church. Even then, they'd probably put a fence around her grave and *Visitor* on her tombstone so that people would know to tiptoe around her in search of the people who *belonged* in Dry Creek.

"Well, it's a beautiful bouquet anyway, with all that baby's breath and green stuff," Linda declared as the others nodded and started to slip away. "And those rosebuds are perfect. You could even take some of them out of the bouquet and press them between the pages of a thick book. They'd look real nice tucked in a big family Bible."

Barbara didn't want to admit that she didn't own a Bible, family or otherwise. She'd moved around so much in the past few years that she didn't even have a cookbook, and she was more likely to use that than a Bible— which was saying something, because most of the hotel rooms where she and Neal had lived hadn't had kitchens and a person didn't need a cookbook to figure out how to heat up a can of soup in a beat-up old coffeemaker.

But a lot of people in Dry Creek valued the

Bible and Barbara wanted them to think she belonged here.

"Thanks, that's a good idea," she replied to Linda and smiled a little vaguely. "Maybe I'll do that."

Before long, everyone had left her side. The bad part about the crowd around her thinning was that Barbara could see the sheriff again. He hadn't moved when all of the people had surrounded her, he'd just waited for them to leave. She wondered what his problem was. If his frown was any indication, Sheriff Carl Wall would be the last one to accept a cup of coffee from her even if she *did* manage to pour a cup.

Chapter Two

Sheriff Carl Wall knew he couldn't arrest someone just for their own good, but he was sure tempted. He was standing here watching Barbara Strong, and she had just gotten the attention of every single ranch hand at the wedding reception. Not much escaped the eyes of those mangy fellows, and they had all noticed that she'd caught the bridal bouquet.

Until today, the sheriff had been able to warn everyone off Barbara, saying she was still in shock over what had happened with her ex-husband. After all, it wasn't every day a woman woke up and found out she was married to a thief. The older people in town had agreed with him, and everyone had decided to give Barbara at least a year to catch her breath. No one was going to put any extra strain on her for at least that long. No requests for volunteer help. No urgent need for favors.

The sheriff trusted the older people in town to keep their word.

He didn't trust the ranch hands. One of the older women, Mrs. Hargrove, had added her voice to the sheriff's when he'd talked to the men about giving Barbara a year of peace. Many of the ranch hands had had Mrs. Hargrove as a Sunday-school teacher in their younger days, and they didn't want to cross the older woman, even though it had been many years since they'd sat in her class.

The sheriff made it clear that he felt it would disturb Barbara's peace if she had to brush off countless pleas for dates. The ranch hands had reluctantly agreed that Barbara might need a little time to heal before she had to start figuring out which man among them to marry next. They'd said a year sounded about right—unless, of course, the woman herself seemed unwilling to wait that long.

The sheriff had thought he was doing good to buy her a year. He'd agreed to the terms.

But now Barbara had just destroyed all his efforts when she'd caught the bridal bouquet. She should have just stood up on a chair and announced her intention to start looking for a new husband. She'd probably get a dozen proposals before the night was over.

The sheriff shook his head. He was tempted to tell the ranch hands that the woman they were ogling was being watched by the FBI. *That* would slow them down. Not that it was strictly true. The FBI wasn't watching her; they'd asked *him* to do that for them.

It seemed Barbara's ex-husband, Neal Strong, might not have been content with robbing gas stations. The FBI suspected he might also have joined forces with two other men to rob some bank down in Wyoming. One of the other suspects, Harlow Smith, was in jail in Billings along with Neal, but the third man was unidentified and still free.

The FBI didn't have any real evidence that Neal was in on the bank robbery, but even though the robbers had covered their faces with ski masks, his body had a strong resemblance to a drawing one of the bank tellers had made of the men. The FBI figured that if Neal was in on it, he would give himself away by trying to do something with the $150,000 in cash that was missing. At the very least, they figured he'd lead them to part of the money through his ex-wife.

So far, the sheriff had watched Barbara closely but noticed nothing. He knew how much she earned at her job at the bakery, and she was barely spending that. She sure wasn't spending any extra stolen money. The only thing she had purchased besides groceries was the school supplies she'd bought for her children. He knew because Barbara didn't have a car and Mrs. Hargrove gave her a ride to Miles City to buy groceries. It all checked out.

The sheriff frowned again. The most suspicious thing Barbara had done was what she was doing now. She'd taken that bridal bouquet and was using it as a fan. It wasn't hot inside here, but Barbara's cheeks were all pink and flushed like—

The sheriff followed the direction of Barbara's eyes. He should have known. She was looking directly at Pete Denning. Or Pete was looking at her. The sheriff wasn't sure who had started looking first.

Pete was the worst of the lot when it came to the ranch hands. He flirted. He broke hearts. He would dance with a cactus if that was the only thing he could find to put his arms around. Rumor had it that Pete had been claiming he was ready to get married these days, now that his good friend Judd was tying the knot. The sheriff had known Pete for years. He figured the ready-to-marry line was just Pete's latest pick-up bait.

But Barbara wouldn't know that. Women just couldn't resist a no-good ladies' man who said he was ready to settle down.

Pete had obviously decided to forget about the year of grace for Barbara. He had probably already said his line to her now that he was standing closer to the woman. That must be why she was fanning herself so hard the rose petals were beginning to fall off that bouquet she held. She probably wanted Pete to know she was listening to his talk about his new-found desire to settle down.

Of course she was listening, the sheriff told himself. Pete was the kind of guy women liked. That was the worst of it. Even when Pete had played a huge mouse in that Nutcracker ballet last Christmas, women had swarmed around him afterward like he was the hero of the piece instead of the villain. Women just naturally thought Pete was exciting.

The sheriff felt himself fade into the background a little bit. He'd long ago made his peace with the fact that women found him dull. They knew he was trustworthy, of course. Women always voted for him for sheriff. But women didn't look at him the way they looked at Pete.

The sheriff knew he didn't understand women. He'd never had much reason to understand them. He couldn't remember his mother. He had grown up in an endless cycle of institutions and foster homes. He'd always been more of a number than a name.

There had never been much demand in adoption circles for a stocky, plain boy who was average in just about everything, so he'd stayed in the state system.

Still, the sheriff was content. He had his job and he was a good sheriff. He understood doing his duty much more than he understood things like being part of a family. Married couples baffled him. Young children made him nervous. But it was okay. He'd found a place for himself in life and it was a fine place.

He'd even made himself a home of sorts on a piece of land outside Dry Creek a couple of years ago. The twenty-acre plot he'd bought had a few trees on it and a creek that ran across the upper northwest corner. The creek wasn't much more than mud in the fall, but in the spring, like now, it ran full and sweet.

The sheriff had bought a used trailer and set it on a foundation close enough to one tree so he'd have shade in the summer. Then he'd built a wooden porch that reached out a good ten feet from the main part of the trailer. The trailer was two bedrooms and, with the porch, felt like a house. Last spring, he'd put a white picket fence around the trailer to keep the deer away from the corn he had planted next to the porch.

Yes, the sheriff thought to himself, he was doing fine.

It's just that he didn't believe in pretending to be something he wasn't. And he wasn't a family man. He could count on one hand the times he had sat down to eat with a group of people when he was growing up and felt like he was eating with a family.

Still, he'd come to peace with who he was. He'd learned some lessons the hard way, but he was a decent, strong man. He might have limitations, but he knew what they were. He wasn't a touchy-feely emotional kind of a man like most women wanted. But that was okay. He knew the importance of duty and he knew how to keep the people in his care safe.

Someday, the sheriff hoped, he'd meet a woman who would appreciate the solid nature of his personality. Of course, she'd probably be a bit dull and colorless herself. He'd figured that out long ago. Whoever she was, she wouldn't be anything like Barbara Strong.

Just look at the woman. She stood there waving that pink-rose bouquet around and looking like a Valentine greeting card doing it. Her dark hair was all curly around her head, and her brown eyes flashed. Her skin was all flushed, and she had a dimple. And it wasn't just her looks that made her seem so feminine—it was the graceful way she fluttered her hands when she talked.

The sheriff could watch her hands talk for hours. He'd noticed long ago that she'd taken off her wedding rings, both the gold band and the diamond engagement ring that went with it. He knew that some women started wearing lots of other rings when they took off their wedding ring, like they were uncomfortable with having the ring gone. But not Barbara. Her fingers stayed bare and her hands moved even more freely with no ring at all.

The sheriff frowned a bit more deeply. Maybe Barbara just didn't have any other rings to wear. That didn't seem right either. A woman like her deserved the best of everything.

She certainly deserved better than to have her heart broken by Pete.

The sheriff sighed. It wasn't always easy looking out for other people. Not that he gave this kind of special attention to everyone who moved to Dry Creek. It was just that he'd started feeling responsible for Barbara when he'd tracked her down to that Colorado hospital after her ex-husband beat her up last fall. He'd sat by her hospital bed for the simple reason that she'd taken one look at him and asked him to stay.

Of course, she might not have been in her right mind when she'd asked him to stay. She'd been drugged with enough pain medication to confuse anyone. For all he knew, she thought he was Elvis or the hospital chaplain or some long-lost purple rabbit from her childhood. But, he'd stayed with her anyway.

When people were drugged, as Barbara had been in the hospital, they tended to mutter to themselves about all kinds of things. While he sat by her bed, the sheriff had heard enough of what was in Barbara Strong's heart to know she dreamed of romance and poetry and knights on white horses. His hopes had sunk with each fanciful dream she shared. She was the kind of woman who would take one look at him and know he didn't have a clue about any of those things she was dreaming about.

The sheriff hoped the day never came when Barbara looked at him too closely. He knew it hadn't come while she was in the hospital, because on the last day of her hospital stay, she'd kissed him. On the cheek like a thank-you kiss. It had been because of the drugs still in her system, he was sure of that. But he'd kissed her back anyway, and not on the cheek. His had been no thank-you kiss, and he hadn't had the excuse of being on any kind of medication.

Barbara had been surprised.

The sheriff had been stunned. He had no excuse for his behavior. He knew he wasn't the kind of man that Barbara dreamed about. He had nothing to offer a woman like Barbara. He didn't even talk about the things women liked to hear. He'd watched Pete flirt with women and realized he didn't have a clue how to go about something like that.

No, he'd always known Barbara would want someone better than him long-term. But that didn't mean he couldn't protect her until she got back on her feet. He meant for her to have her year of peace. He needed it and she needed it, too. She certainly didn't need someone like Pete tormenting her.

The sheriff started moving.

"You got the registration updated on that old pickup of yours?" Sheriff Wall asked as he finished walking over to Pete. When he started asking the question of Pete, the sheriff was standing beside the other man. By the time the question was ended, the sheriff was standing in front of Pete, half-blocking the view the ranch hand had of Barbara.

"Excuse me, ma'am," the sheriff turned and nodded his head toward Barbara. She did look pretty, but he couldn't be distracted. She smelled nice, too. "This will just take a minute."

"That's all right." Barbara smiled at the sheriff. "I need to check on the children anyway."

The sheriff nodded again as Barbara stepped away.

"What'd you do that for?" Pete complained when Barbara was out of earshot. "Now she's going to think I live outside the law like that no-good man she used to be married to! I sent off for the official registration. I told you that when old Charley sold it to me. I've got the temporary permit in my pickup."

By the time Pete had finished explaining himself, both men were standing side-by-side, watching Barbara walk through the crowd of people. Barbara wasn't tall, but she walked tall with her shoulders thrown back and her step confident. She made quite the picture in the lavender bridesmaid's dress she was wearing. The dress had a full shiny skirt that swished and swayed when she walked. If people would only stop talking, the sheriff knew he'd be able to hear the dress.

There, the sheriff thought in satisfaction. A fair number of people had stopped talking. It was almost quiet.

It took a minute for Sheriff Wall to realize what all that silence meant, and he looked around. He didn't have to look far to see a dozen other single men also watching Barbara as she walked across the room to the refreshment table. He scowled at those other men.

"I was just getting ready to ask her out," Pete complained softly.

"That's what I figured," the sheriff said as he gave the ranch hand a friendly pat on the back and turned to walk away.

"Hey, don't you want to see the temporary permit?" Pete called after him.

"Naw, that's fine." The sheriff thought maybe he should get himself a cup of punch from the refreshment table. Just to let the other men know he was keeping an eye on things.

Chapter Three

❧

"Congratulations!" Mrs. Hargrove said as Barbara stopped in front of the refreshment table. Mrs. Hargrove had a long cake knife in one hand and a streak of lemon filling on the white apron she wore over her green gingham dress. The older woman had her gray hair pulled back into a black velvet bun catcher and she wore a pearl necklace.

"Thanks." Barbara thought the older woman looked a little tired despite her finery. She knew Mrs. Hargrove had seen her catch the bouquet, but she didn't want the older woman to have any unrealistic expectations. "Lizette is the one who needs the congratulations though—she's the bride—she was just having some fun throwing her bouquet. She knows I'm not interested in getting married again."

"Oh, you can't give up hope, dear," Mrs. Hargrove said as she sliced another piece of cake and put it on the last clear plastic plate from what had apparently been a stack in front of her. "You're only twenty-nine years old—that's much too young to give up hope."

"Age has nothing to do with it," Barbara said as she caught sight of her children and noted they still seemed to be having a good time playing with the other children. "Marriage just isn't for me."

Not that she was against marriage in general, Barbara thought. She was here celebrating a wedding, after all. And she believed that some people had good marriages. She'd seen couples right here in Dry Creek who seemed very happy. But somehow Barbara doubted that kind of marriage was going to happen for her.

"Not all men turn out to be thieves," Mrs. Hargrove said as she cut another piece of cake and lifted it in the air. Mrs. Hargrove was cutting into the spare overflow sheet cake that Lizette had made because she wanted everyone to have all the cake they wanted. Most people had already eaten a piece of the tiered cake. Mrs. Hargrove looked around to see if there was a plate for the cake she now held on the silver server.

"They don't all turn out to be faithful either." Barbara knew this was at the core of why she didn't believe she would ever have a happy marriage. A happy marriage required a lot of trust, and Barbara had none left. She didn't think she'd ever trust another man with something as important as her heart. But that was okay. A woman could live a fine life without a husband.

Barbara could see there were no plates left for the cake Mrs. Hargrove held. She looked down and saw an open box peeking out from under the white tablecloth. "Here, let me get some more plates for you."

Barbara bent down.

"Oh, no, I'll be fine," Mrs. Hargrove glanced around until she saw the sheriff. "Carl, come here and get these plates so Barbara doesn't have to."

"They're not heavy," Barbara said as her

fingers closed around a stack of plastic plates. She knelt down. Unfortunately, the sheriff's fingers closed around the same stack of plates. He didn't look as though he intended to let go.

"Really, I can get them. It's not like they're gold-rimmed china or anything," Barbara protested. Her voice sounded muffled because her head was half-covered by the white tablecloth as she knelt, but she'd thought she made her point.

Apparently she was wrong.

The sheriff knelt down, too and put his head under the tablecloth to look at the plates. He still kept his grip on the stack of plates. "Everything doesn't need to be fancy. Sometimes the plain old ordinary things are best."

"I know. That's what I'm saying," Barbara continued. She wasn't going to give up that easily. "The plates are plastic. Not fine china. They're not worth anything."

No one would steal them, she added to herself silently. You don't need to worry about me taking them.

She wondered if people would talk later about her and the sheriff snapping at each other under the cake table at Judd and Lizette's wedding reception. She hoped not. The one person she had thought would be her friend when she moved to Dry Creek was the sheriff, but it hadn't worked out that way.

She never did know all that she had said to him when he sat beside her hospital bed in Colorado. She knew she was out of it for some of the time. But the rest of the time, she thought they were becoming friends. She'd loved listening to him talk. He'd told her story after story about Dry Creek, some of them from the days when the cattle first came to the area and some as recent as last spring when he'd picked chokecherries for Mrs. Hargrove so she could make jelly to enter in some contest at the state fair.

Barbara had thought at the time that not many men would pick berries so an old woman could win a prize with her jelly. That's when she'd kissed him. It had been impulsive. Sort of a tribute to what a nice man he was. Then he'd kissed her back—really kissed her.

The sheriff was the one who had driven Barbara back to Dry Creek when the hospital said she could go home. She had no home and no car left, since Neal, not content with putting her in the hospital, had taken a sledge-hammer to her parked car. Her children had been staying with Judd so she'd been grateful for the ride.

Barbara had no choice but to accept the sheriff's offer of a ride. And she'd decided at the time that it was just as well. She needed to gently explain to him that, as much as she had enjoyed his kiss, she was never going to marry again and she didn't want to lead him on to expect a certain kind of relationship when all she could offer him was friendship.

Barbara had her words all picked out and she had decided, with a man's pride being what it was, that it was best to let the sheriff bring up the subject of the kiss.

She had worried for nothing. The sheriff never mentioned the kiss. Once they were back in Dry Creek, he'd become all official and formal around her. He acted like she was a stranger—an unkissed stranger at that.

At first, she'd thought maybe he had a girl-friend and he'd been worried that she might misinterpret the kiss, but she'd soon learned there was no girlfriend. No, he must have just been concerned she would read too much into that kiss for the simple reason that it didn't mean anything to him.

Well, he hadn't needed to worry. She knew the kiss didn't mean anything. She didn't *want* it to mean anything. Still, she thought he could have at least brought the subject up. No kiss was all that meaningless. She had gotten the message back then and she got it now.

"You're a guest here," the sheriff finally said as he gave another tug at the stack of plates.

Barbara let him have the plates as she moved her head back so she could stand up. "No more than everyone else is a guest."

Mrs. Hargrove smiled at Barbara when she stood. "That's better—you wouldn't want to get frosting on that pretty dress of yours."

Barbara nodded in defeat. A person couldn't force acceptance. She wondered if she'd ever really find a home here. Before she could belong, they needed to trust her at least a little. It was disheartening that they wouldn't even let her touch the plastic plates. She could forget about something as advanced as pouring coffee.

She felt like one of those birds in a gilded cage. It wasn't just that no one let her do anything for the community. She was an outsider in the most basic of ways. No one burdened her with their troubles, even though they all knew hers.

On a day like today, Barbara would have liked a friend to talk to about the wedding, but friendship went both ways. She wouldn't ask a stranger to care about how hard today was for her when no one shared their troubles with her.

She was lonely.

Barbara had known she'd have to listen to Judd and Lizette recite their wedding vows today. She'd been prepared for it to be hard, but she hadn't expected it to be as hard as it was. She hadn't been able to listen to those vows without counting all the times her ex-husband had broken his. Talking to a friend would have made that hurt easier to bear.

"Not all men are like your ex-husband," Mrs. Hargrove said adamantly as she lifted another piece of cake and set it on the plate the sheriff was holding out to her. She then turned her attention back to Barbara. "Carl here's a good boy."

Barbara almost laughed at the startled look on the sheriff's face. She wasn't sure if being called a "boy" was the surprise or if he was shocked anyone would think of him as a husband prospect for a woman whose ex-husband was a criminal.

Barbara wondered if that was why the sheriff had never brought up the subject of the kiss. He was probably dismayed he'd kissed the ex-wife of a thief.

Mrs. Hargrove seemed oblivious to the sheriff's reaction as she kept talking to Barbara. "Just give yourself a year or so and you'll meet someone nice."

Barbara shook her head. There weren't enough years in eternity for that. "I have the kids to think about instead."

She looked over at her children, but she didn't walk away from the refreshment table. She'd give herself a minute to pull her thoughts together. She didn't want the children to sense her unhappiness.

The wedding was bringing it all back to her. It had taken her years to end her marriage to Neal, despite the fact that he had started cheating on her almost from the beginning.

When she had tried to talk to him about it, he'd become abusive and accused her of being boring and not open to having any fun.

She'd remembered thinking at the time that it was hard to have fun when they never had the rent money and never stayed in one place long enough to make a home. No, she'd given up on fun. What she hadn't given up on was having a father for her children and a faithful husband for herself. She had kept trying to make Neal into that man, but she'd failed miserably.

"I don't suppose you've heard from your ex-husband?" the sheriff asked Barbara as he passed a plate of cake to someone on his left.

"I've got nothing to say to him."

The sheriff shrugged. "Ever wonder if he has something to say to you?"

So she was right, Barbara decided. It really was her ex-husband that was making the people of Dry Creek hold back on accepting her. Well, there was nothing she could do about it. She'd already divorced the man. That should tell people what she thought of him.

"I should go check on my children." Barbara walked over to where the children were playing a game of hide-the-spoon. She'd initially counted on having her children by her side during the wedding reception today, but when they'd asked to play with some of the other children, she couldn't refuse them. Just because she was uncomfortable at weddings, she didn't want them to miss out on a good time.

Barbara waved at Amanda and Bobby. They both grinned up at her and waved back, but they didn't stop what they were doing.

There was a chair by where the children were playing and Barbara sat down.

What she needed to do was lighten up, she told herself. After all, if she weren't here for a wedding, she would have enjoyed being in the community center again.

The community center was really an old barn that had been donated to the people of Dry Creek. Tonight, it shone with polish. Mrs. Hargrove had organized this reception and, in Barbara's opinion, she'd done a wonderful job. Barbara had offered to help, but everyone had said she should just take it easy. Tables had been scattered across the wooden plank floor, and they were all draped with white tablecloths.

The air smelled like a mixture of coffee and crushed rose petals. There was a hint of lemon too, but Barbara couldn't decide where that aroma was coming from. Maybe it was from the filling in what remained of that five-tiered cake.

The weathered high rafters made the barn look vaguely like a cathedral, especially with the iridescent white streamers that a couple of high-school boys had strung from them. The night outside was dark, so there was no light coming from the open windows, but rows of small twinkle lights circled the inside walls of the barn. A late-March breeze coming in the windows made the streamers sway a little. Yes, it was all very dignified and very bridal.

The wedding ceremony had taken place earlier in the town's small church, and then people had walked over to the barn for the reception. Lizette and Judd were still shaking hands with people.

Barbara realized she might never have a real home with the people of Dry Creek, but she had no question that she had a family with Judd. When she had tracked Judd down, she was desperate for help. She didn't even know Judd back then, but she had no other family and she'd never lived anywhere long enough to make real friends.

The separation from Neal hadn't been going well. After she'd finally found the courage to leave him, she suspected he would try to find her, and hurt her and she didn't want the children to be with her if that happened. Barbara needed someone to care for the children while she made the trip to find them a shelter.

Barbara knew it was not love that had made Neal angry when she'd told him she was going to divorce him. No, he might not want her to divorce him, but he didn't love her. Neal hadn't just cheated on her once or twice. He'd made it a habit. Barbara hadn't known about the robberies he'd been involved in until later, but she had faced the fact that something in Neal had changed dramatically over the years.

Barbara was only twenty-nine years old, but the day she'd left Neal she'd felt like an old woman. It was as if she'd lived an eternity, and nothing had turned out the way she had hoped it would.

It was odd that it wasn't until she finally found the courage to leave Neal that she found the closest thing to a family that she'd ever had. Judd had invited Barbara and her children to stay with him indefinitely.

Barbara figured it was his new-found religion that made Judd so eager to help them, but she didn't think it was a good thing for him to do. Family did have limits. And life wasn't lived in a church. She hadn't had much experience with God, but she had wondered sometimes if God even knew what went on in the world. He certainly had never paid any attention to what went on in *her* world.

No, Judd and his new wife wouldn't find life as simple as they thought it would be. Marriage never was. Barbara knew all of the things that could go wrong with a marriage and she didn't want to be responsible for any of them happening to Judd.

That's why, now that he was getting married, Barbara had moved off Judd's ranch and into the small town of Dry Creek. Lizette had offered the room at the back of her dance studio as a temporary home for Barbara and the children until they found something more permanent. There weren't any houses for rent in Dry Creek right now, so Barbara knew she'd have to wait. Not that there would be any houses for rent soon.

The only house that wasn't occupied was the old Gossett house, and Mr. Gossett was in prison. Mrs. Hargrove wrote to him regularly, and in her last letter she'd asked him if he'd be willing to rent the house. He wrote back saying he was thinking of giving the house to his nephew, but he'd find out if his nephew was interested in renting it out to her.

Even if the Gossett house did become available, it would take a lot of repairs before anyone could live in it.

In the meantime, the room in the back of Lizette's dance studio had become the resting place for Barbara and her children. The room wasn't large, but it was bigger than most of the hotel rooms where they'd lived for periods of time over the past few years. Lizette had lived in the back room of her studio before she got married, and there was a kitchen and a bathroom attached to it. It would be fine.

There wasn't much furniture in the

studio's back room and Barbara had vowed that, now that she and the children weren't moving so much, she would replace that old folding table with a solid kitchen table, the kind of table children needed for family meals and homework.

They might not have a home yet, but they'd have a table. It was a start.

And, for now, the back room was convenient for Barbara since she was temporarily working in the fledgling bakery that Lizette had started in the front part of the building. Barbara knew she'd eventually need to get a job that was more solid, but she was grateful for the bakery job. It was helping her gain some job experience and it was early-morning work so she was done by the time the school bus came through Dry Creek to drop the children off after school.

Barbara ordinarily kept a close eye on her children, but she was checking them even more frequently of late. She'd had these funny feelings the past few days that someone was watching her and the children through the storefront windows. Whenever she looked up, however, she didn't see anyone on the street outside the window, so she was probably being foolish.

Besides, even if someone was looking in the window, it didn't mean anything was wrong. People looked in storefront windows all the time, she reminded herself.

Maybe it was just hard for her to get used to their new home, Barbara told herself. It had bigger windows than most places she had stayed. She wasn't used to so much openness.

At least Lizette had hung good, thick curtains on the windows in the back room. There was no chance anyone could look through those windows when Barbara and the children were sleeping.

Barbara shook herself. Now, why was she worrying about this when she was here to celebrate a wedding? Dry Creek wasn't the kind of place where people went around looking into the private windows of other people. They might be very interested in her and the children, but no one would actually spy on them.

There must just be a draft in that old bakery building and a tingle of cold air must blow through now and again and hit her on the back of the neck, she decided. That must be what that tingling sensation was all about.

Or, she thought to herself, maybe the tingling had just been her nerves reminding her of the upcoming wedding. She'd certainly had reason enough to dread the event.

But now that the wedding was over, the nervousness would stop and that would be it. She could get on with earning the acceptance of the people of Dry Creek.

It was too bad that she couldn't begin with the sheriff. Of all of the people there, he suddenly looked like he would be the hardest to win over.

Chapter Four

The wedding reception was still going strong. Laughter and chatter filled the old barn. Barbara watched the sheriff while she sat in a folding chair beside where the children were playing.

The sheriff seemed to be intercepting anyone who was walking toward Barbara. One would think she had a big *C* for "criminal" branded on her forehead. The sheriff took one man by the arm and pointed him in a different direction. He whispered something in the ear of another. She couldn't imagine why he cared if the ranch hands talked to her. They certainly didn't have anything she could steal.

Well, no matter what his reasons were for keeping people away from her, today was supposed to be a happy day and Barbara was determined to keep looking happy even if she had to change her view to do so.

Since no one was going to talk to her inside the building with the sheriff blocking the way, Barbara decided to go outside. Barbara looked down at the bridal bouquet she still held. Was it just her, or did the flowers look a little wilted?

Sheriff Wall watched Barbara walk back over to Mrs. Hargrove and say something before heading toward the barn door and going outside. Ordinarily, he wouldn't need to follow Barbara everywhere, but if anyone was going to make contact with her, they would do it at some event like this. Strangers stood out in Dry Creek on an ordinary day, but tonight a dozen strangers could wander around and no one would pay much attention to them as long as they held a plastic cup filled with Mrs. Hargrove's special raspberry punch.

Of course, he wasn't worried about Barbara seeking to contact her ex-husband's criminal partners. The sheriff had talked with her enough in the hospital and then later in Dry Creek to know she wasn't likely to turn to crime. She'd seen first-hand what crime did to a person, and she knew it wasn't good.

But that didn't mean Barbara might not unwittingly receive a message from her ex-husband and not realize what it meant. She'd said she hadn't heard from him, but she might be hoping for some message anyway. After all, the two of them had been married for a long time and had children together. They probably still had business to settle between them.

Yeah, the sheriff told himself, he'd better go outside and stand in the dark with her just to be on hand if anyone came up to her with a message. It could be something as simple as "look in the tool chest for the key to the safety deposit box" or "dig up grandma's favorite rosebush and see what you find."

The sheriff wished again that he had some of Pete's charm with women. At least Pete could go out and stand there without looking like a fool with nothing to say.

Barbara took a deep breath the minute she stepped outside. She looked around and was relieved no one else was close by. It did look as though someone was sitting in one of the pickups parked by the barn, but that was the only sign of life. Most of the cars were over by the church. The moon was out, but it was still dark enough that she couldn't see much beyond the vehicles.

Whoever was in the pickup seemed to be taking a nap, so Barbara felt alone enough to relax.

After living through a cold winter here, she knew she'd never get tired of Montana spring nights. They were such a relief after the snow. It was a warm March, and the sounds from inside the barn were muted enough that she could almost hear the sounds of the outside. Now that spring was here, there was no snow to muffle the night sounds. She heard the sound of a coyote off in the distance. And a dog barking closer to town.

Someone had lined up some folding chairs along the side of the barn, and Barbara stepped over to them and sat down. She set the bouquet down on the chair next to her and slid her shoes halfway off her feet. She wasn't used to wearing high heels any more and they pinched. Barbara leaned back in the chair. Now she almost felt good enough to smile for real.

She heard the sound of a pickup door being opened. Apparently, the man was finished with his nap.

Right then, the door to the barn opened and light spilled out into the darkness.

"Trouble?" Barbara asked when she looked up and saw the sheriff. She'd given it some thought and had almost decided that the reason the sheriff had been frowning so much was because he had official business somewhere. Maybe his mood had nothing to do with her. Maybe she'd just grown so distrustful of men that she saw betrayal and censure everywhere she looked.

Yes, that must be it, Barbara told herself in relief. Someone must be in trouble and the sheriff was passing the word along to others who could help. The sheriff seemed always to be working. Even though he was wearing a regular black suit and not his uniform tonight, he was probably still on duty. She supposed a lot of his social evenings were interrupted like this.

"Trouble? No," the sheriff said as he let the door close behind him. He stood still for a moment. "Unless you've seen something?"

Barbara refused to be disappointed that the sheriff wasn't worried about someone else. "Me? What would I see?"

"Oh, you never know when someone sees something out of the ordinary." The sheriff walked over to the folding chairs where Barbara sat and stretched out on the chair closest to the barn door. It was six chairs away from Barbara.

"No, nothing out of the ordinary here."

Maybe the sheriff was just worried from habit, Barbara decided. She was glad she had nothing to worry him further. She had noticed that whoever was getting out of the pickup had changed his mind and settled back into the seat. But there was nothing unusual about one of the men around here deciding to take a bit longer with his nap. A lot of them worked hard and were tired. The only thing that was unusual lately was that strange tingling sensation she'd had at the back of her neck. "Has anybody thought of getting a big streetlight around here?"

"A streetlight? We only have the one street."

"I know, but it's a very dark street—especially at night."

"People like it that way. If they get a streetlight, they worry they won't be able to see the stars."

"It could be a small light."

The sheriff shrugged. "The county is voting next month on all the business. Bring it up at the town hall meeting we have. See what people think."

"Me? Would I go to the meeting?"

"I don't see why not. This is where you live, isn't it?"

"Yes, but—" Barbara had never voted in a local election before. She'd never been in one place long enough to qualify for anything like that. She'd gotten a library card once, but that was all.

"There'll be a vote for sheriff coming up," he added. "If you're interested in voting, that is."

Barbara was relieved. Whatever was troubling the sheriff, he must not suspect her of anything. He was asking her for something that implied she was almost one of the citizens of Dry Creek. "Well, you can count on my vote—I mean, if I don't need to own property or anything."

"Nope. No property. Just show up at the barn here and vote."

Was it really that simple? It wasn't pouring coffee, but voting had to count for something. Maybe becoming part of life in Dry Creek was possible after all. Barbara felt a rush of enthusiasm at the thought. "I suppose you have a campaign team already lined up?"

She knew the sheriff was reliable and did a good job. He'd saved a life or two and he'd even tracked her down last fall. She'd heard enough talk around to know he was well thought of in Dry Creek.

"Campaign?" the sheriff looked startled.

"Yeah, you know, your campaign to get peoples' votes. I'm just wondering if you have anyone working on the campaign. I could help pass out flyers or something if you need someone else to help. Just let me know who to talk to about it."

There, Barbara thought. It was the perfect place to start. A flyer was wortn less than even a plastic plate, so no one needed to trust her with anything. Unless, of course, the sheriff thought she wasn't good enough to hand out his flyers. Maybe since she'd been married to a criminal, he was afraid that she would taint his campaign.

Barbara held herself still. "That is, if you want me to work with you?"

The sheriff felt his collar get tight and he swallowed. He should have worn his uniform instead of this suit. He'd never given any thought to a campaign. People around Dry Creek didn't need a campaign to know to vote for him for sheriff. For one thing, there was no one running against him. But Barbara didn't know that, and if she was working on a campaign with him, she'd have to spend time with him. That would keep her away from guys like Pete.

It would also be easier for him and the FBI to keep an eye on her. Now that he thought about it, it was almost his duty to spend as much time as possible with Barbara Strong.

The sheriff took a deep breath. "Sure. We could get together for dinner tomorrow night at the café and work out a campaign strategy." His voice sounded a little strained, but he hoped Barbara wouldn't notice. He seldom asked a woman out on a date. Not that this was a date. At least, he didn't think it was. "I'd buy, of course."

"Oh, no, I couldn't let you buy—"

"No, it would be official campaign business."

Barbara pinked up for a moment and then she nodded. "Well, then, yes—I'll ask Mrs. Hargrove to sit with the children while I step over to the café. But she might not be able to since it's Saturday night and she needs to get ready to teach Sunday school the next morning."

The sheriff couldn't help but notice how pleased Barbara looked. He could hardly keep his mind on Mrs. Hargrove. He sure wondered if this was going to be a date. But in any case, Barbara was right. They needed someone to watch the children.

"I'll talk to Mrs. Hargrove," the sheriff said.

"That's right—I forgot you know her pretty well. She said you fixed her roof a couple of weeks ago."

"Just a few shingles. Nothing much," the sheriff said. He didn't want to derail the conversation by talking about Mrs. Hargrove's chores. He knew there had to be a chore on her list that was worth a night's babysitting even if it was a Saturday night. "Linda has a great steak special going on Saturday nights."

"She might agree to let us put some of your flyers in the café, too," Barbara said.

The sheriff swallowed. "We sort of need to make a flyer before we can pass it out."

Barbara brightened even more at that. "You mean no one's done a flyer yet? Would it be okay if I worked on that, too? We'll need a slogan. Something catchy. Something that sets you apart from your competition."

The sheriff felt his mouth go dry. He couldn't not tell her. Not when her face was getting so excited. "About my competition… so far I don't have any."

The sheriff closed his eyes.

"Well, surely someone will run against you," Barbara said. She frowned a little. "They probably just haven't put in their name yet."

The sheriff sat up straighter. She was right. Someone could decide to run against him. It wasn't likely, but it could happen. Maybe there'd even be a write-in campaign. One or two people usually wrote in a name on the ballot instead of voting for him. The name was usually Daffy Duck or Santa Claus, but legally it was a vote for another candidate. That had to mean something. He moved a couple of chairs closer to Barbara without even thinking about it. "It's a good thing we're going to do a campaign then."

Barbara smiled. "It's always good to get out the vote. It helps the whole community. We need to think of things that would rhyme with Sheriff Wall."

"There's *all*," the sheriff said, noticing that Barbara had picked up the bouquet she'd caught and was holding it in her lap. He slipped over onto the chair next to her.

"And a button, we'll need a button," she said. "Something in blue. People trust blue. Or maybe red. Red is power."

The sheriff nodded. He didn't care if Barbara decided to dress him up in a clown suit and have him pass out suckers in front of the café. She was sitting next to him and talking and her hands were going a mile a minute.

Saturday night was definitely going to be a date if the sheriff had anything to say about it. He smiled his best smile. "I appreciate anything you can do—for the campaign, that is."

"I'm handling the bakery while Lizette and Judd are gone on their honeymoon, but I can think about the slogan while I work." Barbara held up the rose bouquet as though she was seeing it for the first time. "And, another good thing about this campaign is that it will help people forget I caught this thing."

The sheriff couldn't ask what the first good thing was. He had a bad enough feeling in his stomach about the second good thing. "Why is that?"

"Everyone talks during a political campaign. There'll be issues and answers. People will forget I caught the bouquet and that I'm supposed to be the next one to marry. People think Lizette knows I'm hoping to get married again and that's why she tossed me this bouquet. But I've told Lizette it's just the opposite. I'm never going to get married again."

"Oh."

Barbara stood up. "I'm going to be a good citizen though."

"You can be a good citizen and married at

the same time." The sheriff thought he should point that out.

It was too late. Barbara was already opening the door to go back inside the barn.

Barbara looked around when she stepped back inside. She felt better than she had since she'd come to Dry Creek. This was the perfect solution to her problem. If she campaigned for the sheriff, people would surely see that she took a firm stand in favor of law and order.

Granted, it wasn't like being asked to do a fundraiser for the school or anything that involved money, but it was a start. The next thing she knew, she'd be asked to join the Parent-Teacher Association. Then maybe they'd ask her to pour coffee for the town at some event.

She was so excited. She really was going to make a home for herself and the children here in Dry Creek. And, maybe while she campaigned for the sheriff, she'd mention to people that the town needed a streetlight. That showed even more civic spirit. Eventually, she'd have a normal life with a house of her own.

And, just so she'd know the real house was

coming, she'd work on getting herself that kitchen table for her and the children. It was time she learned to cook something besides sandwiches, and time they started having Sunday dinners at their own table. Fried chicken would be good. Or maybe a pot roast. Having Sunday dinners together was something Dry Creek families did, just like they hung their sheets on the clotheslines in the summer to dry.

Barbara had noticed a clothesline behind Mr. Gossett's old house. It had fallen down, of course, just like most of the things around the house. The good thing about the Gossett house, though, was that it had a picket fence around it. The boards weren't white any longer and they weren't all standing straight, but a coat of paint and a few well-placed nails would change that. She didn't know what she'd do if Mr. Gossett wrote and said his nephew wanted the house so he couldn't rent it out.

No, that wasn't true. She did know what she'd do. She'd just keep looking. She was going to make a home here or, at least have the satisfaction of knowing she'd done everything possible to make it happen.

Chapter Five

Meanwhile, in the pickup truck parked in the night shadows outside the barn, Floyd Spencer had been watching Barbara and the sheriff and muttering to himself. His timing had been lousy ever since he'd robbed that bank with Neal and Harlow.

It'd been his first robbery and he'd since decided that he just didn't have the stomach for crime. Everything had turned out badly. His two partners were behind bars and they were likely to turn informant on him next week if he couldn't get a message to them and let them know that he needed more time to get their money into those off-shore accounts.

He had buried his own money in his

backyard so deep that even his dog couldn't find it. He was too nervous to move it inside under his bed. He didn't know when he'd ever have the courage to dig it up.

But it was the other men's money he had to worry about first.

Floyd had been watching Neal's wife off and on over the past two weeks to see if she ever went to the prison to see Neal. If she did, Floyd would try to get her to take a message to her ex-husband about the additional time he needed to open those off-shore accounts. The message couldn't be anything obvious, of course, or the people at the jail would stop it from getting to Neal.

Floyd couldn't spend too much time watching the ex-wife, however, because he didn't dare call in sick to his job at the bank. He hadn't planned on the whole thing taking so much time.

It had all sounded so simple when Harlow had planned it. But, these days, Floyd couldn't even take a long lunch at the bank. It hadn't been *his* bank that had been robbed; Floyd wasn't that stupid. But it had been the bank in a nearby town, and the jittery nerves had spilled over to his bank. He hadn't thought about that happening.

Everyone was watching everyone these days, and Floyd sure didn't want to make anyone suspicious enough to remember that he'd called in sick on the day the other bank had been robbed. He had thought it would be easy to do everything Harlow had asked. But it wasn't as easy as Floyd had thought it would be to transfer money into those accounts without anyone knowing about it. He'd found the instructions to make the transfer, but he didn't see how it could be done secretly. Harlow and Neal had each set the accounts up in partnership with another person so, even in jail, they said they would be alerted when the money was in the accounts.

Floyd didn't know how all of that was to happen. He was a bank cashier, not a thief— well, until now, that is. All he knew was that Harlow was clever enough to do whatever he said he was going to do and Neal followed the other man's directions. Harlow had been the one who'd talked Floyd into helping them rob the bank. He would never forgive Harlow for that. Robbing that bank had been the worst mistake of Floyd's life.

But there was nothing to do about it now except to go forward and try to find some time alone with Neal's wife. If she wouldn't help him, Floyd thought he'd take a day off work and try to impersonate a clergyman going to visit Neal. It was a long shot, but who else would care about Neal except someone who was paid to care, like a minister?

Floyd didn't know what he'd do if he couldn't take time off work. Maybe he should leave some money for Barbara Stone at the bakery just in case he needed to go to his back-up plan.

Floyd vowed that if he got out of this mess, he'd never break any laws ever again. He wouldn't even cross the street against the light. He'd come to the conclusion that his nerves just weren't good enough for a life of crime. He couldn't sleep. He'd barely eaten since he'd helped rob that bank. Once he got the money into those offshore accounts, he planned to go to a hypnotist and try to get the memory of what he'd done wiped out of his mind.

Chapter Six

Barbara's alarm clock went off at five o'clock in the morning and she groaned as she reached over to turn it off. It was dark and her children were still asleep. Fortunately, it wasn't cold inside the room she now called home. Not that it was warm either. She sat up on her cot and pulled a blanket around her shoulders.

Her alarm clock gave off a green hazy light so Barbara could see the two lumps in the bed next to her cot. Both Amanda and Bobby were curled in on themselves as they slept. They'd been tired enough last night that they would sleep another few hours.

Barbara yawned as she remembered last night.

The wedding reception had become more enjoyable after she had asked to work on the sheriff's re-election campaign and she'd spent more time talking with Mrs. Hargrove about local politics. Mrs. Hargrove had gotten so involved in the conversation, she hadn't seemed to notice that Barbara was helping clean up the refreshment table.

The two of them had cleared off the cake crumbs and picked up empty punch cups while they talked. Barbara had learned enough about local politics to know that she probably didn't need to campaign for the sheriff to win the election.

Of course, Mrs. Hargrove encouraged her to work on the sheriff's campaign anyway.

"Campaigning is more like fun than work, isn't it?" Mrs. Hargrove had anxiously asked her for the second time as she looked over to where the sheriff stood.

Barbara had nodded.

"Well, then I guess it's okay—it's a great way for you to meet people. Besides, it never hurts to remind people to vote," Mrs. Hargrove said as she turned her attention back to the table and scraped some white frosting off the cake knife before wrapping the knife in a wet paper towel.

"I'd enjoy it," Barbara said. "Really I would. I want to do something for the community."

Mrs. Hargrove nodded. "We've become a little lazy around here when it comes to voting for the sheriff. And it's an important job—we can't have just anyone as our sheriff. I've known Carl Wall since he was a teenager, and he's a good man."

Mrs. Hargrove finished her wrapping and stood to face Barbara. "You know, now that I'm thinking about it, I'm not sure we give the man enough recognition for the job he does. And here he is risking his life day after day to see that we're all safe. Why, he could take a bullet any time and here we sit, not even having the courtesy to go vote for the man."

Barbara had lain awake last night trying to wrap those words of Mrs. Hargrove's into a snappy campaign slogan—something like "Vote for Carl Wall. He'd take a Bullet for Us All." Last night she'd thought that slogan had possibilities. This morning she wasn't so sure.

Oh, well, she thought as she stood up. Even if it was Saturday morning and Amanda and

Bobby wouldn't be getting up quite yet, she certainly needed to get moving. The first thing she needed to do was to make three dozen donuts for the display case at the Dry Creek café. Then she needed to make six dozen maple donuts for the Martin ranch, six assorted fruit pies for the café in Miles City, and—well, she'd need to check her list for the other two orders. She knew one of them was a dozen corn muffins for someone and the other was a sour cream raisin coffeecake.

The bakery business was booming in Dry Creek.

Lizette was starting out small. She was only taking direct orders and she advertised that they'd fill any order as long as it met the minimum order amount of fifteen dollars. Delivery was an extra charge, but it was small enough to encourage business.

All of the items were made fresh every day. The only things a person could buy without a pre-order were the donuts that Linda stocked in the café. Every morning, the bakery sent three dozen donuts over to the café. Lately, if they had time, they'd added a pie or two as well.

The bakery was building up a steady stream of regular customers, and Barbara was pleased that Lizette had felt comfortable leaving the business in Barbara's hands during Lizette's honeymoon. When she returned from her honeymoon, she had said she planned to devote most of her time to her small dance studio and turn most of the bakery duties over to Barbara.

As Barbara wrapped herself in her robe and walked to the bathroom, she planned her day. If she started now, she should have the bakery orders done by nine-thirty this morning. Mrs. Hargrove had volunteered to go with her as she delivered the orders since Barbara didn't know her way around some of the back roads yet and didn't have a car to drive anyway. Neal had seen to that.

Barbara told herself she wasn't going to think about Neal today. She'd enjoy the drive with Mrs. Hargrove. Amanda and Bobby would both enjoy a ride out to some of the ranches as much as Barbara would.

If she got a minute, Barbara decided she'd even take a few of the flowers from that bouquet she'd caught and press them between two boxes of sugar. It wasn't a book, but the boxes should give enough weight so the roses would press down good.

The sheriff always checked Mrs. Hargrove's house as he drove into Dry Creek in the early morning. He didn't have to go out of his way, because Dry Creek only had the one main gravel road that went through the little town and he went straight down it. Mrs. Hargrove's house was on the left, a few houses down from the café. The sheriff checked to see that her kitchen light was on when he looked at her house.

The sheriff knew the older woman would be indignant if she knew about his daily checks, but he'd started to worry a few years ago about her living alone. Seeing a light on in the kitchen eased his worries. He figured that if Mrs. Hargrove could get downstairs to the kitchen, she was doing all right. If the light wasn't on when he drove by at seven o'clock, he'd make a swing back around nine o'clock. If it wasn't on then, he'd call her on the telephone with some question or another.

It wasn't often that Mrs. Hargrove's light

didn't come on before nine. This morning, though, there wasn't a light on anywhere in her house when he drove by at nine. The sheriff figured she was just tired from the wedding reception last night, so he decided to wait another half hour before he called her. This time he even had a good excuse. He needed to ask her what chore he could do in exchange for a Saturday-night babysitter.

In the meantime, he should call and check in with the FBI.

Not that there was ever anything new with the FBI. He'd report that there'd been no suspicious activity from Barbara Strong and they'd report that Neal and Harlow were still in jail and looking more hopeful than they had any right to be. Neal had even asked for a calendar yesterday. There'd been some debate about whether or not having access to the correct date was a constitutional right, but, in the end, it had seemed harmless to give him a calendar.

The sheriff shook his head. He knew about people's rights and he was all in favor of respecting them, but he wasn't inclined to do any favors for a man like Neal Strong. A man that would hurt a good woman like Barbara and the two little ones...well, a man like that didn't need to know what day of the month it was.

Barbara had the maple bars all boxed up and the pies cooling on the table next to the triple batch of chocolate chip cookies the Elkton Ranch had ordered. It was nine-thirty in the morning and she was ready to start her deliveries. She'd thought Mrs. Hargrove had said she would drive by the bakery and pick her up at nine o'clock. Barbara took another look at the street in front of the bakery. There was still no sign of the older woman.

"Can I take my bear with me?" Amanda asked as she came out of the back room.

Amanda had already asked to take her Raggedy Ann doll and her princess doll.

"You can only take one toy with you, but it can be any one you want," Barbara said.

"Bobby's taking a book to read," Amanda offered. "A big one. One he can read all by himself."

Barbara recognized the hint of jealousy in her daughter's voice. "You'll be able to read those big books right alongside him pretty soon."

One of the reasons Barbara wanted to make a home for the children here was that they needed more stability in their lives. She wished Dry Creek was large enough to have its own school, but the one in Miles City was good and the children were happy there. Since today was Saturday, they had the whole weekend to be with her. They would enjoy their weekend, but they wouldn't fuss on Monday when they got ready for the school bus.

Barbara heard the phone ring and thought it must be Mrs. Hargrove calling. Maybe her car wouldn't start or something.

"Hello, Dry Creek Bakery," Barbara answered the phone. The phone was for bakery business, so she always answered it that way even if it was after hours and she knew it was a personal call. "Can I help you?"

"I'd like to order a cake," a man's voice said.

The voice sounded muffled, as though the man didn't want anyone to overhear him. Calls like that had come to the bakery before, for surprise birthday parties, so the voice did not alarm Barbara.

"We can do a special design for you—or a special cake. What kind of cake would you like?"

"A patience cake."

Barbara frowned. "I don't think I've heard of that."

Barbara could hear what sounded like office noise in the background.

The man's voice got even smaller. "I looked on the Internet. It's got coconut filling inside and yellow cake outside."

"Well, I can certainly make a yellow cake with coconut filling for you."

The man's voice was down to a whisper. "It needs to say it's a patience cake."

"We could put a card with the cake that says it's a patience cake." Barbara figured the cake was to remind some usually cranky boss somewhere to be patient on his birthday. It occurred to her that there weren't many offices within their delivery area. She should probably check. "Our usual delivery only goes into Miles City."

"I'll pay extra if you take it to Billings."

Barbara hesitated. "We'd have to charge an extra forty dollars to cover the gas. I'm not sure it's worth that to you. I can give you the name of a bakery in Billings if you want."

"Last night I left two hundred dollars for you under that wooden planter on your porch."

"Here?" Barbara was starting to get that tingling feeling on her neck again. Why would anyone be leaving things on her porch at night?

Barbara took the phone with her as she walked over to the door and opened it. There was only one planter on the porch and it was empty. The geranium had died during the winter. Barbara lifted up the planter.

"There's three one-hundred-dollar bills here."

"Yeah, that's like I said. I must have given you an extra big one without thinking. Is that enough?"

Barbara was silent. No one around here paid three hundred dollars for a cake even if it was very special. Or very big.

"How many people does this cake need to feed?"

"Just one."

Barbara was silent. People around here also didn't mistakenly leave an extra hundred-dollar bill anywhere. Most of them didn't even carry hundred-dollar bills. "You've paid too much money. Even with delivery to Billings, the whole thing won't be more than eighty dollars."

"You can keep the change."

"Oh, that wouldn't be fair—"

"I want to send a message, too, so it's not just the cake," the voice continued. "Do you have a pen to write it down? It's important that the words go just the way I say them."

Barbara walked over to the counter where the phone message pad was. "Do you want a singing telegram or someone to deliver your message in a costume or something?"

She was still trying to figure out why so much money had been left on her doorstep.

The man cleared his throat. "No, it's just the message. Here it is. 'Be patient. God's preparing riches in glory for you next week. This cake comes from your spiritual brother—who, but for the grace of God, would be where you are now.'"

Barbara wrote down the man's message with a frown. "You don't want to say 'Happy Birthday' or anything?"

"Should I?" the man whispered.

If Barbara hadn't been holding three hundred dollars in her hand, she would think this was a joke. Not a funny joke, but a joke of some kind.

"Where do you want the cake delivered?"

"I don't know the exact address," the man hesitated. "But I know who. He's in jail in Billings. Name of Neal Strong."

"What?" Barbara held her breath. This had gone beyond weird. The only sensible explanation was that someone was playing one of those cruel jokes on her. It had to be one of her Dry Creek neighbors. No one else knew who she was. "Who are you?"

"Please, just take him the cake." The man hung up the phone.

A minute went by before Barbara heard the sound of a car outside. She looked out the window, expecting to see Mrs. Hargrove's old car.

Instead, she saw the sheriff's car. He drove a white sedan with the county insignia on the door and a siren on top.

She'd never been so glad to see the man, and that included the time when she was in the hospital and he was the one to remind the nurses that she was due another shot for her pain.

"Look at this," Barbara said, holding out the pad of paper. The sheriff was standing in the open door to the bakery. She'd been so rattled she hadn't even closed the door when she'd come in from the porch earlier.

Sheriff Wall looked at the words Barbara had scrawled on the notepad. The first thing he saw was *Neal Strong* at the bottom.

"Someone said they wanted to send Neal a—a cake," Barbara stuttered. Her face was white. "A patience cake with coconut filling."

"I see." The sheriff didn't know how much to tell Barbara. She might be better off not knowing that this was probably the contact the FBI had been expecting.

"He made it sound like he was some kind of religious person. Called himself a brother. But he's not. I mean, I don't know much about religious people, but this guy is creepy. Nothing like Pastor Matthew over at the church."

"Oh, no, I don't suppose he is anything like Matthew." The sheriff wasn't a regular churchgoer, but he knew he would be sitting there this Sunday, right after he finished helping Mrs. Hargrove with her Sunday-school class. Mrs. Hargrove drove a hard bargain. She had agreed to babysit so he could take Barbara to dinner tonight, but she had named her price.

The sheriff was to help Mrs. Hargrove with her class of first- and second-graders and then sit through the church service that followed. He'd rather have reroofed her whole house than help her with her Sunday-school class. He'd even offered the roof. She'd said no.

Then he had pleaded ignorance. He'd mentioned his childhood with all the foster homes and never a Sunday-school class. He didn't have a clue about how to help her. He couldn't even remember ever hearing about Sunday school. He didn't even know what they did there.

Mrs. Hargrove had a hard heart. She didn't bend with his panic. She said that if he didn't know what went on in Sunday school, it was high time that he learned. Then she said he'd have the whole church service after the class to recover from Sunday school anyway.

The sheriff was glad he'd gotten to know

Pastor Matthew over the years. At least a man like that might have something worth listening to during the church service.

"I don't think anyone has any business ordering a cake for Neal." Barbara folded her arms, then looked at the back of the room. "Oh, the children—"

Barbara stepped away from the sheriff and smiled at the children who had slid soundlessly into the room, dragging blankets and toys with them. They both stood still, looking at their mother with big eyes.

"There's nothing to worry about. Someone just wanted to order a cake. Go in the back and get your jackets on for when Mrs. Hargrove comes to drive us on the deliveries."

The sheriff cleared his throat. "Mrs. Hargrove slept late this morning. I'm going to help with the deliveries."

Barbara nodded. "It'll just take me a few minutes to put together a cake. Lizette keeps some sheet cakes in the freezer, and we have some coconut filling in the cupboard."

The sheriff noticed that Barbara kept the smile on her face until the children had gone into the back room.

"You're actually making a cake for this guy?" the sheriff asked.

Barbara nodded. She held out the three one-hundred-dollar bills. "I don't know if these are real and I don't know who ordered the cake. Even if it's just some sick joke, I can't have people saying the bakery isn't filling the orders they take over the telephone, especially when—if these bills are real— someone left money for it. I told Lizette I'd take good care of the bakery while she's gone. I won't let her down. I'll just put the man's change back under the planter where he left these."

The sheriff took the bills from Barbara and looked at them closely. "They look real to me." He looked up. "I don't suppose he left the bills in an envelope, did he?"

Barbara shook her head. "Why?"

"We might be able to trace an envelope— you know, fingerprints and all."

Barbara shook her head again. "You could try to get fingerprints off the bills."

"Too many prints. It'd drive our guys crazy trying to pick them all out."

"Well, he didn't do anything illegal by

ordering the cake," Barbara said. "It's not very nice, but that's about it. It has to be a joke—I mean, I can figure that out. Although I thought everyone here liked me well enough…"

The sheriff hesitated. The FBI had made it clear that the decision about whether to tell Barbara Strong that she might receive a message for or from her ex-husband was the sheriff's to make. If he felt Barbara needed to know for her own safety, he could tell her.

The sheriff didn't think Barbara was in any physical danger, but he hated to see that stricken look on her face.

"I mean, I know people are probably talking about me a little bit because of Neal, but—" Barbara's voice sank so low the sheriff could barely hear her. "Well, Neal's not the best person and I know I did marry him and I suppose it might seem like a funny joke to play on me to have me deliver a cake to him when he's in jail."

Barbara was looking down at the floor. She had that expression on her face that the sheriff remembered from when she was in the hospital.

"It's not a joke," the sheriff said as he put

out his hand and lifted Barbara's chin until he could see her eyes. He tried not to be distracted by the soft feel of her skin or the tears that were gathering in the corners of her brown eyes. Why did brown eyes always make him feel so protective? He didn't remember that he used to feel that way.

The sheriff let go of her chin. He needed to. "Don't worry about it."

"Well, it might be more of a prank than a joke," Barbara mumbled. "And I know newcomers can expect some of that kind of thing. I just didn't think that in Dry Creek—"

"It's not anyone from Dry Creek," the sheriff said. The woman didn't know how to stop fretting, and he couldn't stand to see her cry. He hoped he was doing the right thing to tell her. "It's probably a message from one of your husband's friends."

"My husband doesn't have any friends," Barbara said and then she swallowed. Her eyes got big. "Oh, you mean—"

The sheriff nodded. "He apparently didn't work alone all of the time."

"But why would they send a message through me? I don't even visit Neal."

The sheriff nodded. He knew that. "Maybe that's why they're paying you to make the cake and take it."

"Well, I won't do it now. I'll just put all of the money back under that empty planter with a note that we can't make the cake. No one would expect the bakery to bake a cake for a criminal."

The sheriff hesitated. If Barbara delivered the message, whoever it was who had been working with her husband would most likely leave her alone. But, if she didn't deliver the message, the man might not be so happy with her. "I think its best just to do what he asks. At least, until we find out who he is."

"Neal doesn't even like coconut," Barbara said as she took the hundred-dollar bills back from the sheriff. "I don't suppose you have five twenties?"

The sheriff shook his head.

"Well, if I'm going to make the cake, I'm going to charge for it. Lizette can use the business. I quoted the man eighty dollars, including delivery, so that's what I'll charge. I'll need to get some change from the café." Barbara started walking toward the porch.

"Is there anything I can do to help?" the sheriff said. He was relieved to see that Barbara's tears had gone.

"Watch the children while I go over to the café and get change."

"Me?" the sheriff asked, but Barbara had already left the room.

When the sheriff had asked if he could help, he'd thought more along the lines of—well, when he thought about it, he realized he hadn't had any specific actions in mind. But, if he had, they wouldn't have anything to do with watching little children. The sheriff knew about juvenile delinquents—he'd lived with some until he turned eighteen—but he didn't know anything about the crop of sweet little kids that was springing up around Dry Creek these days.

Fortunately, the children didn't know he was unprepared to deal with them. Bobby and Amanda had both come out into the main room carrying their jackets and looking at him cautiously.

The sheriff forced himself to smile. The children didn't smile back. They just stared at him.

The sheriff reminded himself that the children were going to be adults someday. There couldn't be that much difference in the conversation of a child and an adult. He just needed to pretend they were a little older.

"Doesn't look like it's going to rain today like the weatherman said," he remarked. "You'd think that the weatherman would get it right more often than he does."

Bobby and Amanda continued to stare at him. He could have been speaking a foreign language.

"Makes you wonder if there's some sort of weatherman's school," the sheriff finally continued. "Of course, a weatherman's school wouldn't be like the one you go to—how is school going anyway?"

The sheriff could kick himself. He did know that no child liked to be asked about school. He'd hated that question himself. "Not that it's any of my business," the sheriff added. "I'm not checking to see if you've done your homework or anything. It makes no difference to me. Now, whether or not you go to school, that's my business. I can arrest you if you're truant. But homework—"

The sheriff could see Bobby's eyes grow large.

"Can you put people in jail if they don't do their homework?" Bobby swallowed. "I was going to do it. Honest. But I forgot."

"I don't want to go to jail," Amanda added. Her lower lip started to tremble and she wailed. "I can't even read the big books—not like Bobby can."

"I'm not here to arrest anyone," the sheriff assured them both. He needed to stop the conversation before he had them both in tears.

"My princess doll doesn't want to go to jail either," Amanda said with a sniffle as she dropped the jacket that had been over her arms and showed him the doll that had been hidden under the jacket. "Only bad people go to jail. Bad people like my daddy."

The sheriff swallowed. He wondered if it was too late to make another comment about the weather. If he'd been talking to an adult, he might have done just that. But Amanda and Bobby were children, and all children deserved to think the best they could of their fathers.

"Your daddy did something bad. That's why

he's in jail. He's not necessarily a bad person," the sheriff explained. "People sometimes do things that they shouldn't—or don't do things that they should. Then they're sorry for it."

"I promise I'm going to do my homework. It's just that I don't understand the math questions," Bobby said as he looked up at the sheriff. "They talk about peaches."

"Don't worry about your homework," the sheriff said as he put his hand on the boy's shoulder. That seemed to calm Bobby. "It's okay if you don't do it."

The sheriff realized he should have kept an eye on the open door.

"No, it is not okay," Barbara said as she came back into the room with some twenty-dollar bills in her hand. "He has to do his homework. Don't tell him he doesn't need to finish his homework."

"I didn't mean—" the sheriff mumbled. "Of course, he needs to do his homework, it's just that it's not a crime if he doesn't."

"It's a crime around here."

The sheriff surrendered. He'd never be able to explain. "Yes, ma'am."

"I'm not a 'ma'am,'" Barbara protested. "A

'ma'am' is someone like Mrs. Hargrove. And she's in her seventies."

The sheriff was beginning to wish he was in jail himself. Except then he would have missed the picture Barbara made with her dark eyes flashing and indignation making her cheeks rosy. He smiled and ducked his head. "Well, you're not like Mrs. Hargrove, that's for sure."

The sheriff thought of adding that he'd never had the urge to kiss Mrs. Hargrove on the lips, but he thought he'd better not say that.

Barbara's eyes stopped flashing, but her cheeks stayed rosy. The sheriff couldn't stop staring at her. She was a picture.

Everyone was quiet for a minute.

"I still don't understand about the peaches," Bobby finally said.

"I could—that is, well, if it's the peaches that are the problem, I could help you with them," the sheriff offered. He forced himself to turn his eyes to Bobby. "Just to be sure you get your homework done."

The boy smiled. "It's subtracting."

The sheriff nodded. "We'll figure it out—why don't you bring it along while we deliver the bakery stuff? You can ask me questions on the road."

The sheriff figured a few questions would keep his mind off the boy's mother.

Bobby nodded.

"I don't have any peaches," Amanda said. She moved a step closer to the sheriff. "But I have a princess. See?"

The sheriff nodded. The girl looked just like her mother must have at that age. He wanted to pat her on the head.

"You can't see from way up there," Amanda said.

The sheriff knelt down so he could admire the princess doll. "Well, you're right, she's very pretty, isn't she?"

Amanda nodded. "And she's going to learn to read big books, too. It won't be hard for her 'cause she's a princess."

"I'm sure she's going to learn to read all kinds of books just fine," the sheriff agreed. "Just like you will."

"You'll learn to read better next year," Barbara said as she walked toward the back room. Amanda had not gone to kindergarten so she was behind some of the kids in the first grade class, but the teachers assured her she would catch up. "I'll just be a minute with that cake."

"Take your time, ma'—" the sheriff floundered. "I mean, Mrs.—that is, Barbara."

The sheriff couldn't help but remember the days in the hospital when he'd called Barbara "dear." Of course, she was so confused from all the pain medication at the time that she'd never even reprimanded him. She probably hadn't even heard him.

There was nothing wrong with her hearing now. Barbara turned around and frowned as she walked through the doorway leading to the back of the building. "I'm not a Mrs. anymore. Barbara is fine."

The sheriff watched her go into the other room. The woman was more than fine. "Yes, Barbara."

The sheriff wondered if Barbara had any idea of how very perfect she was. Probably not. Unless, of course, someone like Pete Denning had already begun to tell her. The sheriff wondered if the thought of Pete sweet-talking Barbara should trouble him as much as it did.

He sure hoped he wasn't falling for Barbara Strong in a serious way. He had a feeling it would take a long time to get her out of his system once she married someone else.

And, of course, that's what she would do. A woman like her could have her choice of the single men around here. One of them was bound to strike her fancy. The sheriff would be a fool to hope otherwise. His days of calling Barbara "dear" were long gone. He'd be calling her "Mrs. This" or "Mrs. That" before he knew it, so he'd best not think of her as anything but "Barbara."

The sheriff sighed. He sure wished he could go back to calling her "dear."

But the sheriff never was one to grieve over what couldn't be helped. He just needed to do something to meet more women. There was bound to be someone sensible whom he could date. Maybe he'd meet someone in Miles City. As he recalled, Charley had a niece somewhere in Miles City who was single. Maybe he should ask the older man to set up a blind date for him.

The sheriff sighed again. That's what he should do all right. But maybe he'd wait until he got this stuff finished with Barbara and her children first. Then he'd be able to concentrate on dating someone.

Chapter Seven

The sheriff had never been on his knees around children. Apparently, Amanda and Bobby got under his skin as much as their mother did. "Maybe we should talk about some of those peaches about now."

The sheriff needed to get back to something familiar, and homework about peaches would do as well as anything, especially if it was math homework. Math was clean and reasonable. A man knew when he had the right answer. There was no guessing at what something meant or wondering if there was a better way to say something.

The sheriff felt like he didn't know anything. Knowing the answer and helping a boy with his homework were two different things. The sheriff knew he shouldn't just give Bobby the answer to the question, so it took him twenty minutes to help Bobby think through how many peaches Howard would have left to enter in the best peach contest at the state fair if he started with eighteen, then sold four before he got there, ate three himself and gave one to each of five friends he met on his way to the fair.

Bobby had a question about whether Howard was supposed to give a peach to everyone he met along the way or only his friends. The sheriff didn't know a thing about friends, but he couldn't say that to the boy, not when Bobby was looking at him as though he knew how the sun and stars were hung in the sky. So the sheriff did his best to answer the question the way he thought Barbara would want it answered.

The sheriff acknowledged that if Howard had given a peach to everyone he passed on the way he would have none left to enter in the contest at the fair. So, it couldn't be right to give everyone a peach.

Together the sheriff and Bobby decided

that a peach only really needed to be given to someone who was very hungry. That was duty, the sheriff explained and it was important to do one's duty. Giving the peaches to his friends, well, the sheriff reasoned that was something Howard had done because he wanted to do it. It wasn't related to the job. A wise man, the sheriff counseled Bobby, would look in his basket and count how many peaches were left before he gave them all away.

"But I want to have lots of friends," Bobby said. "Somebody would sure be my friend if I gave them a peach."

The sheriff was exhausted. He felt as if he'd interrogated a dozen prisoners instead of figuring out the fate of a basket of peaches. There was more to homework than the sheriff had expected. And it didn't end with Bobby's peaches.

It took the sheriff another ten minutes to reassure Amanda that she was a smart girl and would learn to read better at the right time and, when she did, that she'd be able to do the kind of homework that Bobby had in front of him right now. And, yes, Bobby would, of course, give one of the peaches to her. Sisters came before friends in the peach line.

The sheriff half expected to feel sweat on his forehead when he rubbed his hand over his face. He wasn't used to talking to children at all. He certainly had never been called upon to help in questions like this.

"I'm ready," Barbara called out from the back room just before she came back out with a triple-layer cake in a square box with a cellophane window.

The sheriff wondered how the woman did it. She was obviously doing a great job of raising her kids. She probably handled a dozen peach questions every day. And she made it all look so easy.

The sheriff rose to his feet when Barbara came into the room. Not only did she raise the kids, she also made one great-looking cake. No wonder Pete was flirting with her. The sheriff could see through the cellophane to the flaky coconut topping of the cake inside. She'd even tied a blue ribbon around the box to make it look festive.

"That's very nice," the sheriff said. He noticed that a long strand of dark hair had escaped the clip that Barbara had used to pull her hair back and away from her face. She was wearing a pressed white blouse and jeans. If she hadn't been carrying the cake box, he was sure her hands would have been gesturing all around. She still didn't wear any rings on her fingers.

"I've got the note right here," Barbara said as she used her chin to point to the card that was slipped under the ribbon. She sounded triumphant. "I copied it word for word. If it contains some secret message for Neal, he'll get it."

"That's good," the sheriff said. The sheriff looked down at Bobby and Amanda. The two children had moved closer to him as he helped them with their homework and they had stood up shortly after he had. Amanda was leaning against his leg and Bobby was standing just inches away from him. The sheriff put a hand on each of their heads. "I guess we're ready to go then."

The sun had risen several hours ago, but it hadn't brought any heat with it. The sky was overcast and the sheriff figured spring would take its sweet time in coming to Dry Creek. It sure wasn't making an appearance today.

The air was cool and a breeze was coming from the north.

Barbara and her two children were gathered with him around his car as it stood parked beside the front steps of Lizette's place. The road came close to the building, but there was a lane left bare for parking and the dried ruts of car tires from previous rains had turned the ground uneven. Everyone was wearing a sweater and the baked goods were packed in the trunk of his car.

The sheriff decided the odds were good that it would rain before the day ended and that was fine with him. If the day got cooler, it would only make the inside of his car feel cozier.

He was glad he had the use of the full-size official sedan. There were no bucket seats in the car and, if Barbara were so inclined, she could slide a little closer to him on the ride back later today after they'd made all of the deliveries.

Something about thinking about all of those peach friends of Bobby's made the sheriff want to draw a little closer to someone. Maybe life wasn't always about having enough peaches to enter the contest.

Barbara's children had slid closer to him this morning when they did their homework, the sheriff reasoned. Maybe it was just a sliding kind of a day since it was cold and gray. Speaking of the children, they would probably be napping in the car by the time they were all driving back from Billings, especially if it was still drizzling outside.

If the afternoon was cold, the sheriff told himself that maybe he'd put on some slow-moving music in his cassette player to make the inside of the car feel warmer. It wasn't poetry, but a man couldn't go wrong with music. Maybe Barbara would slide over and not even realize it. They might even have one of those comfortable conversations they'd had by her hospital bed, those long talks that had been about nothing and everything all at the same time. If they talked like that for awhile, maybe Barbara would forget all about trying to find a husband like Pete Denning.

Yes, a rainy day would be good.

If the sheriff hadn't been dreaming of impossible things, he'd have noticed sooner that they had a problem right here and now that had nothing to do with the weather or peaches or music. It was Barbara who pointed out the problem. There was nothing for the children to sit on when they rode in his car.

"I have handcuffs," the sheriff offered after a few seconds as he bent down to peer into the backseat of his car, hoping to find more than he knew was there. "Of course, they don't lend themselves to much height, but they would keep the kids in place if we cuffed them to the seat straps—"

"You can't put handcuffs on my kids!"

"Well, it wouldn't be for criminal purposes, it would be for their safety in the car."

"I can't believe the county doesn't supply you with booster seats."

"So far we haven't had any prisoners so short they need extra seats," the sheriff said. "If we do start to arrest them, I guess then we'll get the seats."

"I did my homework," Bobby said softly.

"I know you did, son," the sheriff said as he reached over to put his hand on the young boy's shoulders. The sheriff smiled down in the most reassuring way he could. "Like I said before though, it's not an official crime with the state if you don't do your homework some days."

Barbara looked at him a little strangely, but she didn't say anything.

For the first time in his life, the sheriff wished he had a way with children. He knew some men were just natural Pied Pipers. Children followed them anywhere, giggling and smiling. The sheriff wasn't the kind of man whom children considered fun. Look how nervous he'd made Bobby even before they'd talked about peaches. The boy had thought he might be arrested at any minute for failing to do something as simple as his homework.

Of course, the sheriff knew some other things were more important to a child than fun. And he knew he was some of those things. He was reliable and children could count on him. He'd protect a child with his life. That might not be fun, but it was certainly useful if a child was ever in trouble.

The sheriff moved his hand from Bobby's shoulder to his back. He felt Bobby lean into his hand slightly.

Barbara was right, the sheriff knew. Even if it was for safety, he wouldn't stand for someone putting handcuffs on this young boy or his sister either.

The sheriff took off his hat and rubbed his forehead. Barbara and the children were all standing next to him on the left side of the car. The morning air smelled of wet grass. The sheriff felt the crunch of gravel under his boots as he moved around slightly and he heard the sound of a pickup in the distance. He could tell it was an old pickup because of the grinding sound of the engine. The sheriff thought it was too bad he didn't have engine trouble with his own car. That would at least buy him some time.

The sheriff didn't relish explaining his predicament to the entire town of Dry Creek. He was the sheriff; he was supposed to think ahead and be prepared. Now that Barbara had caught that bouquet, he knew people in this town would be measuring the men around her to see who was the best candidate to be a new husband. Pete Denning would probably have thought of booster seats and arrived at Barbara's door with a bouquet of flowers this morning in addition to the seats. The sheriff was more used to solving crimes than anticipating the needs of a family.

The hardware store was directly across the

street from where they all stood and the sheriff could see one or two of the older men stand up so they could see them better out the window.

The sheriff ignored the urge to wave to the men. He didn't want them to take a wave as an invitation to come over. The older men inside the hardware store were always helpful to anyone in town who had car trouble, and the sheriff suspected the men thought it was mechanical trouble that was keeping him, Barbara, and the children outside in the chilly air, looking at the car instead of just climbing in and driving it down the road.

"It's just that Amanda is small for her age and really needs one. Bobby is on the edge so he can get by. But we at least need one for Amanda," Barbara finally said. Her cheeks were pink from the cold and her hair was mussed from the slight wind that had started to blow. "I'll have to get the seats that Mrs. Hargrove uses in her car when she takes us someplace."

The sheriff heard the sounds of the hardware door slamming shut. He hoped that meant one of the men was going to go out to his pickup so he could drive home.

"She'll lend them to you, but don't be surprised if she asks a return favor," the sheriff said. He might not be good at anticipating all of a family's needs, but he did know Mrs. Hargrove. "She's recruiting people to help her with her Sunday-school class tomorrow."

Barbara turned white. Mrs. Hargrove had asked her to bring the children to Sunday school before, but the older woman had never pressed her when Barbara gave an excuse not to accept the invitation. And some of her excuses had been pretty thin. "Maybe instead of helping, I could make her a pie with some of the tart apples Lizette bought before she left. I'm sure Mrs. Hargrove would like an old-fashioned apple pie. Charley said it's the best he's ever tasted."

Barbara had watched the older man as he marched across the paved road from the hardware store to where she stood with her children. He'd obviously been listening to her talk as he walked.

"That's a fact," Charley said as he stepped within easy talking distance. The old man was wearing a red-and-black-checkered wool jacket. The jacket swung open and showed a pale-blue cotton shirt underneath. Charley took another step and was close enough to Barbara so he didn't have to raise his voice to be heard. "I keep saying it was some of the best pie I've ever eaten. Reminds me of the pies folks make around here at Thanksgiving time when the apples are more tart than sweet."

The older man paused for a moment, whether out of respect for the apples or because he was caught up in the memory of a long-ago pie.

Then he gave Barbara a look and started again, "Just for the record, my nephew likes apple pie, too. I wouldn't be surprised if it was a family weakness. If some woman were to make him an apple pie, I reckon he'd propose on the spot. If she threw in a basketful of fresh-fried chicken, he'd even set the wedding date."

"I'm not looking for a proposal—or a wedding date," Barbara said. She smiled at the older man to show there were no hard feelings. "I'm just looking for car seats."

"Well, my nephew could get you the whole car, seats and all. Who has a car without car seats anyway?"

"She means car seats for the kids—booster seats," the sheriff said. He took some comfort in the fact that car seats seemed as bewildering to Charley as they were to him. Maybe Pete wouldn't have thought of them, after all. At least the sheriff seemed to know more than Charley about them. "Mrs. Hargrove has some—we're just thinking about asking her to lend them to us."

Barbara seemed not to have heard anything the sheriff was saying. He heard her continue to mutter to herself.

"I could throw in a batch of donuts. She likes maple donuts," Barbara murmured under her breath.

The sheriff grunted. "I offered to reroof her house so she'd babysit while we have dinner tonight and she didn't agree. That's a thousand-dollar job if she has to hire it out. But she didn't bite. She said she needs extra help with those kids in Sunday school. That was her only trading offer."

Charley chuckled. "She's always looking for help with those kids."

Barbara shook her head. "How bad can they be? They're in Sunday school! I wouldn't think they would dare give anyone much trouble no matter how bored they were."

Charley laughed. "I've never heard any of the kids complain about being bored in Mrs. Hargrove's class. She keeps it all lively."

The sheriff grunted again. "Let's go over to her place. We'll see what she says."

Barbara looked down the street. "I'll have to walk with the children."

The sheriff nodded. "That's what I figured. I'll walk with you then, too. I can carry the seats back here if you agree to her terms."

"I don't think there will be terms," Barbara said. "I'm going to offer to give her a pie."

The sheriff nodded. He didn't want to discourage her, but he had known Mrs. Hargrove a lot longer than Barbara had.

Charley turned to go back into the hardware store. Barbara held out her hands to Amanda and Bobby and started walking. The main street of Dry Creek was made of hard-packed gravel. She felt the stones through the soles of her shoes. She looked over her shoulder at the sheriff. "I don't think she's going to ask me for any favors. I think you're teasing me."

The sheriff caught up with her and smiled. He wished he did know how to tease her. "Yes, ma'am."

"Barbara." She kept her eye on the sheriff as she kept walking. He was enjoying this. She hadn't seen him smile this much at her since she was lying in that hospital bed. The pain medicine she'd taken had made everything vague in those days so she didn't remember many exact conversations that she'd had with the sheriff. But she did remember the feeling she'd had. She'd dreamt he called her "dear" and tucked her in at night. She'd felt safe for the first time in years with him in her hospital room. The fact that he was smiling so much now made her uneasy. It was a dead giveaway that he believed she'd be on the losing end of her deal with Mrs. Hargrove.

Barbara lifted her chin. She'd surprise the sheriff.

Mrs. Hargrove looked as if she was delighted to have the children use the booster seats she kept on a shelf in her garage. "Of course they can use them. That's what neighbors are for—I'm glad you came to me."

Barbara was breathing easier. She and the sheriff were standing in Mrs. Hargrove's yellow kitchen, just inside her back door and next to the bench where people sat to take off their muddy shoes. So far the older woman hadn't mentioned anything about Sunday at all. Of course, Mrs. Hargrove had her hair in curlers so she might still be a little sleepy, but she didn't look as if she was even going to try to bargain.

Barbara decided Mrs. Hargrove probably had all the help she needed with her Sunday-school class since she had Sheriff Wall to help her. What child would be disobedient when the sheriff was there? "I appreciate you letting us use the seats very much."

Barbara glanced over at the sheriff and added, "We have to use them. It's the law."

Mrs. Hargrove nodded. "You'd use the seats anyway. You're a good mother."

"I try to be," Barbara said as she turned to look through the screen door. Amanda and Bobby were both sitting on the back steps of Mrs. Hargrove's house playing with a calico kitten.

Mrs. Hargrove nodded. "That's why I

figured you were just waiting to settle in a bit before you started Amanda and Bobby in Sunday school. I'm sure they will love to come once they start."

"Oh." Barbara didn't know what to say. Mrs. Hargrove hadn't exactly asked her anything so it seemed safest to not answer anything.

"Bobby was asking me about the Red Sea just the other day." Mrs. Hargrove didn't wait for an answer. Her voice was conversational, as though she was just chatting away on a fine spring morning. "One of the other kids had told him about it—you know, the story about when Moses parted the sea and everyone walked through on dry ground. Bobby couldn't figure it out."

"Yes, well—" Barbara cleared her throat and looked over at the sheriff. "He's never seen much water. We went to Devil's Lake in North Dakota once, passed through a town named Whitman, but that's all."

"He was probably just thinking about how much water there is in a lake," the sheriff said. "You know, if ten people poured a gallon into the lake and five people took a cup out, how much lake do you have left?"

Barbara looked over at the sheriff and smiled in gratitude. "Yes, it's probably just something like that."

Mrs. Hargrove nodded. "The boy's a thinker all right. But it wasn't math that was concerning him. It was more along the lines of whether miracles actually can happen."

"I wouldn't want him to be disappointed," Barbara said. She knew all she needed to know about miracles. She knew they weren't for the likes of her. She doubted her children were destined to encounter any either.

"A child needs to know there is Someone who is bigger than their problems," Mrs. Hargrove said softly. "Bobby would like Sunday school. It's the perfect place to look for answers to all the big questions."

"He's too young to have big questions."

Barbara knew she was wrong the minute she heard the words come out of her mouth. Bobby was a seven-year-old boy with a father in prison. He had to have questions. He would probably also want a miracle.

"No one's too young for big questions," Mrs. Hargrove said, as if the matter were settled. "Of course, you'll want to come with him—and bring Amanda, too. And, since you'll be there anyway, you might want to watch the children as they draw a picture of the Bible lesson." Mrs. Hargrove looked over at the sheriff. "Watching the children draw is complete pleasure. It's not work at all."

The sheriff made a funny strangling sound.

"I'm not sure I could be much help," Barbara said. "I don't know what any of the Bible lessons would look like."

Mrs. Hargrove shrugged. "There's usually some camels and sheep. The kids put them in any scene whether they are mentioned or not. It's okay. As long as nobody puts in a car or a flying carpet, that's all we bother correcting. You'll be perfect. Besides, Carl here is going to tell the story, so you'll be able to figure out what the pictures are supposed to look like."

"I am?" The sheriff seemed surprised. "I'm telling the story?"

"I was going to make you an apple pie—" Barbara tried again. She could swear the sheriff looked as if he'd swallowed something sour. That couldn't bode well for Sunday school. "Lizette got some tart green apples from that produce stand just outside Miles City."

"Oh, an apple pie would be wonderful," Mrs. Hargrove said. "And you could take a picture of it with Carl, here, for your campaign. There's something about apple pie that makes folks want to vote. Besides, if you're both there in the Sunday-school class, you'll be able to take more pictures to use in Carl's campaign. It's not exactly kissing babies, but it's pretty close if you take a picture of him with the children. You might even do a press release about it."

"They'll let someone take pictures in church?" Barbara asked. It didn't sound proper to her.

"Sure," Mrs. Hargrove shrugged. "Although this is Sunday school and not church, so it's even less formal. There will be graham crackers and crayons all around."

"I don't know about taking pictures." The sheriff frowned. "Isn't that a little—well, I wouldn't want to seem self-serving."

"This is a political campaign, Carl Wall. You need to be self-serving," Mrs. Hargrove said bracingly. "Besides, people love to see their children in the paper. We might even be able to talk the Miles City paper into doing a feature on your campaign if you offer the Sunday-school pictures."

"People want to know I can fight crime, not that I can pass out crayons to six-year-olds."

"People want to know that you have this community's best interests at heart," Mrs. Hargrove declared. "There's no better place to prove that than in my Sunday-school class."

Mrs. Hargrove sent both Barbara and the sheriff a look.

Barbara nodded meekly. She doubted Mrs. Hargrove needed the sheriff in her class to maintain order.

Barbara looked out the screen door at Amanda and Bobby. Had she misjudged their need for answers to the questions in their lives? They were so young, she had a hard time thinking that they might have questions about good and evil.

"And the pie will be lovely, too," Mrs. Hargrove said as she opened the screen door to lead the way to her garage and the car seats. "I do like an apple pie for Sunday dinner. Maybe you'll have a chance to make it before next Sunday."

Barbara nodded. She'd planned to make a pie for Mrs. Hargrove anyway. The older woman had helped her with many things since Barbara had come to Dry Creek. "I'll make one next Friday or so."

"That's plenty of time. Just don't work on it today. I don't want it to interfere with getting ready for your date tonight," Mrs. Hargrove said cheerfully.

The sheriff's face went white.

"What date?" Barbara asked in confusion. "You must mean our dinner tonight. That's not a date. It's a meeting about the sheriff's campaign."

"Well, whatever it is, I hope you have fun," Mrs. Hargrove waved her hands at them. "And don't worry about rushing through dinner. It's not good for a body's digestion to eat fast."

"We won't hurry," the sheriff said.

Barbara thought the sheriff looked a little grim. He didn't need to look so worried. She knew it wasn't a date.

"I'll go pick up those booster seats," the sheriff added as he stepped outside.

The children followed the sheriff when he went down the steps.

Mrs. Hargrove watched them all walk toward her garage. "Yes, Carl Wall is a fine man." The older woman looked back at Barbara. "He'd make someone a fine—" Mrs. Hargrove paused a moment and studied Barbara's face. "Sheriff. He'd make a fine sheriff."

Barbara didn't know why she was disappointed. She had planned to point out to Mrs. Hargrove just why she, Barbara Stone, didn't care if the sheriff would make a fine husband to some woman or not. Or a fine date either. She had been so sure that was what the older woman was going to say.

And why shouldn't Mrs. Hargrove say it? Barbara asked herself glumly. The older woman was right. The sheriff *would* make some woman a fine husband. He couldn't spend his whole life driving divorced women and their children around in his car. He probably was doing it because it was his duty, anyway, especially now that she'd received the note to pass on to Neal.

"I need to buy a used car before long," Barbara said.

Mrs. Hargrove nodded. "In time. Everything will happen in its time."

Barbara wasn't so sure about that. But she wasn't about to tell the older woman her doubts. Mrs. Hargrove would make her go to Sunday school for more than just this Sunday if she thought Barbara was asking big questions. Barbara's only consolation was that the sheriff didn't seem any more enthused about teaching Sunday school than she was.

Chapter Eight

Floyd reached into his pocket for an antacid pill. He had been standing behind a tree next to this old deserted house, watching Barbara Strong and those kids of hers for the past hour, and they'd spent more time in the company of the sheriff than Floyd thought was necessary. He wondered what they were talking about during all that time. He'd seen that big box with the blue ribbon that Barbara had loaded into the trunk of the sheriff's car. That had to be the cake. At least she had made it.

Floyd put the antacid pill in his mouth to let it dissolve.

And he tried to relax. Fortunately, no one knew he was the one who had ordered that cake for Neal Strong. Even if Barbara told the sheriff about the cake, no one could trace anything to him.

Floyd wondered what he was thinking: he shouldn't be worried about the cake. He should be worried about what would happen to him if the word didn't get through to Neal and Harlow that he needed more time to get their money deposited in those bank accounts.

Even though his two partners were locked up in jail, Floyd had no doubt that Harlow had the connections to see that Floyd was hurt if Harlow thought he'd been double-crossed. Harlow wouldn't leave a bone unbroken in Floyd's body. Harlow had said as much before they committed the robbery. At that time, Floyd had wondered what could go wrong.

Now Floyd knew everything that could go wrong, and he wished he could go back in time and tell Harlow that he, Floyd Spencer, was not the man Harlow needed for the job.

Floyd watched as Barbara Strong, her two children, and the sheriff all left the yard of that old woman's house. Floyd wished he could talk to Neal and Harlow directly and assure them that he was doing all he could.

He didn't like pinning his hopes on a cake.

Floyd looked more closely at the children walking beside Barbara and the sheriff. He could tell by the way Barbara put her hands on the boy's shoulders that she loved him. He supposed even Neal loved the boy.

Floyd thought a minute. He sure hoped Neal loved his son. If the message didn't get to Neal with the cake, Floyd would have to think of some other way to get the attention of his partners. The son was Floyd's best bet. Neal would make sure nothing happened to Floyd if Floyd had his son.

Floyd took a deep sigh. He just hoped everything went okay with that cake. He'd have to go to the jail and see if anyone took that cake inside. If the cake was inside, Neal would get the message. At least, Floyd hoped so.

Floyd took another look at the boy. The kid was kind of skinny, so he shouldn't be much of a problem if Floyd needed some extra insurance. And the girl was small, too, which was good if he had to take them both.

Floyd gave another sigh. He didn't like any of this. He reached for another antacid. If this kept up, he was going to have to get another packet of them. He'd bought this one at a little grocery store next to the motel where he'd been staying in Miles City. At this rate, he'd need to buy another packet tonight.

Chapter Nine

The sheriff was walking down the street away from Mrs. Hargrove's place when he got a bad feeling that this cold gray morning was going to bring him more trouble than it already had. It was about ten o'clock and both booster seats were slung over his back, one resting on each shoulder. Bobby was holding onto the left edge of the sheriff's jacket.

Barbara was walking on the sheriff's other side and she held Amanda's hand in hers. Earlier, the sheriff had tried to balance both booster seats on one shoulder so he'd have one arm to swing in unison with Barbara's just in case she could be convinced to hold his hand to keep her fingers warm. He'd almost dropped both seats before he decided any hand-holding would have to wait for another chilly spring day. It was March, so another day like today would come along soon enough so that wasn't what was troubling him.

No, the bad feeling he had wasn't about the weather. The sheriff wondered if it was nothing more than a sense of being fenced in. He was surrounded by a woman and her children. It was an unusual place for him. Maybe he felt trapped. No, he realized, as he tried the idea on in his mind to see if it fit. It wasn't that way at all.

In fact, he kind of liked this feeling he had, and if this was what trapped felt like, then it was okay with him. A man could get used to being pulled in all directions and having little voices fire off questions at him while he kept his eyes on the ruts in the road just to be sure he didn't lead one of the children to make a misstep that would cause them to take a tumble.

No, it definitely wasn't feeling trapped that was the problem, the sheriff thought as he looked up from the ruts. When he raised his eyes, he saw where the danger really was. It was coming straight at them and moving fast.

Pete Denning was stomping down the street, swinging his arms and muttering things that were probably curses, although the sheriff couldn't hear the actual words so he didn't know for sure. Even from a distance, the sheriff could feel Pete's eyes glare at him. Something was wrong. And, whatever was wrong, the sheriff figured Pete thought the sheriff was it.

A wind was blowing around a few things that rustled and a dog was barking somewhere, but the sheriff still thought he caught the sound of a soft growl coming from Pete's throat—which was odd, since Pete was wearing a white shirt that was so well pressed that it had creases down the long sleeves. It wasn't the kind of shirt that a man would normally wear if he was planning to make trouble. Added to that, the ranch hand's boots were polished until they looked like they'd just come out of the store's box.

Unless the sheriff was mistaken, Pete was even wearing that belt buckle he had won in the rodeo in Miles City last year. That buckle was Pete's pride and joy. He kept it dangling from the mirror in his old pickup, vowing it was too good to wear.

Pete was dressed like he was going to a funeral, but the sheriff was never wrong about the fighting look in a man's eyes, and Pete had that look all over him.

Pete stopped a few yards away from the sheriff and braced his legs.

The sheriff didn't have room to get into a good fighting stance, not with Barbara on one side of him and Bobby on the other. Even if he could get ready to fight, he wasn't about to fight a Dry Creek citizen without knowing what the other man was so agitated about anyway.

"Is there a problem?" the sheriff asked in what he hoped was a friendly tone. Until the sheriff knew Pete's intentions, he wasn't going a step closer to the man. And before he moved, he would see that Barbara and the children were out of harm's way and he'd put down those booster seats on some dry patch of ground so they wouldn't be damaged.

After that, if Pete was still determined to brawl, the sheriff wouldn't back down

"Is it about the permit for your pickup?" the sheriff prodded when Pete was silent.

"You know it's not about the pickup," Pete ground out and then spat on the ground. "It's about you making fools out of all of the rest of us guys. You just wanted a head start. You and your phony year of peace."

"Oh, goodness, what's that?" Barbara asked as she moved up until she was even with the sheriff. She was still holding Amanda's hand. "Is the sheriff's department sponsoring some campaign for non-violence or something? I could make a flyer."

The sheriff had a sinking feeling that he knew what year Pete was referring to. "The sheriff's department always sponsors non-violence."

There was a moment of silence.

"Well, it's only Pete," Barbara finally said as she took a step closer to the man and smiled at him. "How's everything today?"

Pete ground his teeth into a smile. "Good morning, ma'am. Everything's just fine."

"Please, call me Barbara. Everyone does."

Pete nodded at Barbara without taking his eyes off the sheriff. "I'm just wondering if some folks standing here don't call you something a little more affectionate than Barbara."

Barbara gasped. "Why—"

The sheriff lowered the booster seats to the ground and took a step closer to Pete. He motioned for Barbara and the children to step back. Pete looked determined to fight and the sheriff wasn't feeling as opposed to it as he had at first.

Then he heard a boy's thin voice coming from behind him.

"I call her Mommy sometimes," Bobby confessed in a rush. "I know I'm not supposed to—I'm going to start calling her Mom. The other boys call their mommys Mom instead of—well, you know. Now that I'm seven, I'm too old for a Mommy. The other boys told me so."

Pete's eyes softened as he looked past the sheriff and down at the boy. "I wasn't worried about you. I think it's great that you call her Mommy."

"I call her ma'am," the sheriff said. He knew it wasn't always true, but usually it was. "Or Mrs. Strong if it's an official matter."

The sheriff might wish he called her something more affectionate, at least when she was able to hear him, but the truth was that he didn't have the nerve. The only times he had called her "dear," she'd been in the hospital so doped up with pain medication that she wouldn't have heard a drum if it was beating nearby. A "dear" like that didn't count for anything but dreaming.

The sheriff would fight a man if he had to, but he drew the line at fighting anyone over something that hadn't even happened.

"I'm not really Mrs. Strong any more," Barbara offered.

"Well, I'll call you Mrs. or Miss whatever you want," the sheriff said.

It occurred to the sheriff that he'd been a little disrespectful here. He hadn't even asked Barbara if she objected to being called Mrs. Strong. That's what the FBI called her, and he had gotten into the habit of referring to her by the same name. He'd change that though. "Are you going back to your real name? The one you had before you got married? You should let the post office know."

"Forget about names. Can we get back to

our problem?" Pete said from where he stood. "I haven't got all day."

The sheriff could tell the ranch hand was weakening in his anger. Confusion would do that to a man. "I don't have all day either."

"We have to finish delivering the bakery orders so we can meet for dinner to work on the sheriff's campaign," Barbara informed Pete.

Pete frowned. "You're going to dinner together to work?"

Barbara nodded. "I'm helping with a flyer for the campaign."

"So, it's not a date like Charley said?" Pete asked.

"Why would he think that?" Now Barbara frowned. "It's a working dinner. To get the vote out. I thought the men in Dry Creek saw women as equals. You wouldn't object to a man having dinner with the sheriff to discuss the campaign, but the minute a woman does it, you question her integrity!"

The sheriff was a little distracted by the pink flush that anger brought to Barbara's face. He didn't suppose that now was the time to remark on how cute she looked though. "No one's questioning your integrity."

Barbara turned on the sheriff. "He thinks we're going on a date!"

For the life of him, the sheriff couldn't think why that was such a bad idea.

"So, it's not a date?" Pete asked again more cautiously. The ranch hand shifted his weight. He didn't look ready to fight anymore. He did have a grin growing on his face though.

The sheriff wondered how a grin could annoy him so much. "It could be a date."

Pete chuckled. "Not if it's just to get the vote out."

The sheriff grunted. "Nobody votes around here anyway."

"I voted last election," Pete said. His smile grew even wider. "Of course, I voted for Santa Claus."

"Well, you need to vote for the sheriff," Barbara scolded him.

"Why?" Pete said with a shrug. "He's going to get the job anyway. I didn't want to waste my vote."

"Do you know Santa Claus?" Amanda's small voice interrupted.

Pete shifted his feet and knelt down so he

was eye level with the girl. "Well, now, I've been known to write the old fellow a letter or two in my day. I reckon he still remembers me. Did you want me to send him a message?"

Amanda nodded. "Bobby says I'm too old for Santa Claus."

"It's only March. Christmas is more than half a year away," the sheriff said. He didn't like that Bobby had slid away from his side and was now leaning against the ranch hand too. "There's no need to send a message now."

"I don't know," Pete drawled as he winked at Bobby and Amanda. "Like they say, the early bird gets the worm."

"Yuck, I don't want a worm," Amanda said. "Unless it's a princess worm. But it would have to have a crown."

Pete nodded thoughtfully. "With diamonds? I think all princesses wear diamond tiaras. I don't know about worm princesses though. Diamonds would be too heavy for their heads. And they're expensive. Where would a worm get enough money to buy a diamond?"

Amanda giggled. "You're silly."

The sheriff knew before he turned his head

that Barbara was smiling at the ranch hand the same as her children. What was it about Pete, the sheriff wondered, that made women and children like him so much?

The sheriff was beginning to regret that there wasn't going to be a fight. Taking a swing at the ranch hand would make the sheriff feel a lot better about now.

Barbara hadn't heard Amanda giggle very often lately. Pete was right about diamonds. They were expensive. She remembered the diamond engagement and wedding ring set that she had tucked away in her things in the back room of the bakery. She and Neal had bought a matching set of three expensive rings. She wondered how much the two she had would be worth if she sold them. She should get enough money to buy a nice dining room table and chairs.

Barbara would get more if she had Neal's ring to add to it though, because then she'd have all three rings. Maybe she could buy carpet for the floor, too. She wondered what Neal had done with his ring and if he'd give it to her to buy carpet.

After Amanda's giggle faded, Pete stood up again.

"We'd best get going," the sheriff announced.

Barbara nodded. Since she'd probably see Neal today, she'd just flat out ask him for his ring. That was the best thing to do. He certainly didn't need it as a souvenir.

Three hours later, the sheriff sat with his hat in his hands and watched the children. Amanda and Bobby were sitting in a corner of the visitors' area at the Billings prison. Bobby was reading to Amanda from his book.

For the first time all day, the sheriff wished there was someone else to watch the children so he could pay more attention to Barbara as she talked to her ex-husband through the Plexiglas. The sheriff wondered how, since he was sitting so far away from both of them, he was supposed to know that her ex-husband didn't pass her any messages.

Of course, the janitor sweeping back and forth near Barbara and her ex-husband was an FBI man, so the sheriff figured he'd find out soon enough if any messages had been passed. He just wasn't sure he liked the fact that Barbara's voice was low and he couldn't hear what she was saying. He could see that Neal Strong was smiling, and he hadn't even opened the card that went with the cake. No, it sure looked to the sheriff that Neal was smiling just because Barbara was there talking to him.

Barbara bit her lip. She could see Neal's face clearly through the Plexiglas and could tell he was trying to be pleasant. He obviously knew, as she did, that they were being closely watched.

The visitors' room in the jail had tall ceilings and a faint echo. A row of chairs on her side matched the openings in a long counter with Plexiglas windows. It all smelled of cigarette smoke. There were two other visits going on at the same time that Barbara sat there.

"I thought the children would do better with their homework if they had a table to sit at," Barbara said in a low voice. She'd just asked Neal if she could have his wedding ring.

Neal shrugged. His eyes were rimmed with weariness and his face was unshaven. "Sure.

Sell it. I had it on when I came in here. They have it up front someplace."

Barbara nodded. "I'll tell the kids that you wanted to help with the table."

"Yeah, well. Whatever."

Barbara thought she saw guilt in Neal's eyes.

"I didn't exactly plan for it all to end this way," Neal finally said. "They're good kids."

Barbara nodded. "Yes, they are."

"I'm glad you came so I could tell you that," Neal said.

Neal looked over her shoulder and Barbara knew he was watching the children where they sat in the corner.

"I wouldn't have except for the cake," Barbara said. She didn't want Neal to think everything was forgiven and forgotten. She'd never forget.

Barbara had given the cake to the guard when she first arrived for the visit. The sheriff had told everyone about the card so Neal was allowed to have the cake and card. Barbara assumed the FBI was hoping Neal would respond to the card and give them some kind of a tip. But Neal didn't. He didn't even seem to notice the cake.

"The cake has some coconut, but I kept it light," Barbara said. "I know you don't like coconut."

Neal nodded. "Thanks."

"Well, I'm going to be going then," Barbara said. She thought of all of the angry things she had thought she'd like to say to Neal if she saw him again, but now she didn't want to say any of them. He looked so defeated.

Barbara looked around and signaled for the guard.

"Ask him if I need to sign something so you can have what was in my pockets when I came here," Neal said.

Barbara nodded. "Goodbye, Neal."

The sheriff opened the car door for Barbara. The visit with her ex-husband had been fruitless. The guard had reported that Neal had signed over his belongings to Barbara and that she had taken them, but the FBI had already examined everything he had in great detail so there were no new clues there.

"Keep your eyes open for any new purchases though," one of the FBI men had told the sheriff as they whispered outside the jail while Barbara started walking the children back to the car. "That's the only way we're going to know if she's in on any of this."

"Don't you think the fact that she told me about the cake pretty well clears her?" the sheriff asked.

The FBI man had shrugged. "Telling you about the cake got the cake to him, didn't it?"

The sheriff shook his head as he walked away from that discussion. Those FBI men saw too much crime. They'd be suspicious of their own mothers. As far as the sheriff was concerned, Barbara was in the clear.

"Let's get out of here," the sheriff said as they finished walking to the car. Barbara already had the children settled in the back-seat and was opening the door on the passenger side of his car for herself.

Barbara nodded as she sat down in the seat. "I feel chilly."

"I'll turn the heater on in the car," the sheriff said as he sat in the driver's seat. He didn't like the whiteness in Barbara's face.

The sheriff noted that the sky was overcast. He was right about it being a cold afternoon. With the heater going nicely, the children would probably doze off in the backseat before they were ten miles down the road. He didn't have much hope that Barbara would want to slide closer to him and snuggle, though. He only hoped she wasn't going to cry.

Chapter Ten

It was five-thirty in the afternoon when they arrived back at Barbara's place in Dry Creek. All of the bakery items were delivered. Now that they were back, the sheriff offered to carry a sleeping Bobby inside to a bed. Barbara didn't usually have visitors in this back room where she slept with the children, but Bobby was too heavy for her to lift, so she nodded her agreement.

Barbara was the first one through the outer studio and stopped at the doorway of the back room. She winced as she looked around. She wished she'd at least taken the time to paint the room before she'd moved into it several weeks ago. The walls were drab and made everything look worse than it was. Not that drabness was the room's only problem.

"This is only temporary," Barbara told the sheriff as she stepped into the room so he could also enter. She switched on the overhead light, hoping it would make things look cozier. It was late afternoon and dusk seemed to be creeping in earlier than usual, probably because the day was still overcast. The extra light didn't do much for the room in Barbara's opinion. Maybe it would have been better to leave everything in shadows instead of turning on the light in the ceiling. "I plan to find us a real home soon."

The sheriff laid Bobby on the bed. "And what makes a real home?"

Barbara shrugged. "A yard with a white picket fence, I guess. Something solid where the kids can feel secure." Barbara looked at the sheriff and smiled. "At least something with more than one room. They need that."

The sheriff nodded, but his eyes didn't leave her face to look around the room. "That'd be good for all of you."

"I can do it, too," Barbara said. She looked closely at the sheriff so she could judge his reaction. Her ex-husband had never thought she was serious about wanting a home. He had never thought she could do much about it either so it wasn't surprising that she'd given up on even talking with him about her dreams. She wondered if the sheriff knew what a real home would mean to her children.

The sheriff nodded. "You can do anything. You just need a little time."

The sheriff's eyes were a mossy green with golden flecks and Barbara could see that they were serious. He believed she meant what she said. She'd do it, too. "I'll have to work hard. Maybe get a second job."

The sheriff frowned and the green of his eyes darkened. "You don't want to work too much, not with the kids needing you."

Barbara nodded. "That's what has stopped me from taking a second job so far."

The sheriff looked like he was going to say something else, but he didn't. He just ran his hands over his head like he was trying to straighten out his hair. "I need to get Amanda," he finally said as he left the room.

Barbara realized she'd never noticed before what a fine head of hair the sheriff had. First his eyes and now his hair. She wondered why it had taken her so long to see his finer points His hair was an ordinary kind of light brown, but it was thick and looked like it had a nice texture to it. He should really leave his hat off more often, especially in the spring when a hat wasn't needed for warmth or shade. Then people would see his fine eyes and hair.

Barbara would have to mention the hat to him some day when he was more likely to take her advice. No one seeing this room right now would want to take her advice on anything related to looks and fashion. Maybe it was that realization that made her look at the sheriff more closely. For months, she'd thought of him as plain, but maybe he really wasn't. Maybe he was like this room and just needed to make a few changes to bring out his positive points.

Barbara went to the counter that ran along one side of the room and wiped it with a dish towel even though there was no need. The counter was stained, but nothing had spilled on it. The room was clean. It was just also—well, *used up* were the only words that came to mind.

She was wrong in thinking that the sheriff was like this room. There wasn't a positive point to this room, and the sheriff had his share of pluses.

Barbara sat down in a folding chair and rested her arms on the folding table. The table felt as though it could collapse at any time. Everything in the room was old or stained or temporary. None of the dishes matched. The silverware was mostly plastic. Even the lamp by the bed was missing a shade and looked ready for the trash.

A footstep sounded in the outer studio and Barbara looked up as the sheriff entered the room and then carried Amanda to the bed. Barbara wondered when the children had grown too heavy for her to lift. They were changing, just as Mrs. Hargrove had indicated. They were old enough to notice things like not having a proper home.

"I'll be back in an hour," the sheriff said as he pulled a blanket up over the children and looked over at Barbara. "Don't let them sleep too much or Mrs. Hargrove won't have a chance at getting them to bed at a reasonable hour later. By the way, I'll pick up Mrs. Hargrove on my way."

Barbara stood up. "Don't worry. They adore her. They'll probably pretend to go to sleep if nothing else just to please her."

The sheriff smiled and nodded. "I'll be back soon then."

"I'll be ready."

Barbara watched the sheriff walk out of the building. He didn't appear to have noticed how worn everything was, but maybe he was too polite to remark on it. Just as she was too polite to mention that he should stop wearing a hat. She walked over to the stove and turned on the heat under the teakettle.

Barbara shook her head. She needed to forget about the sheriff's hat and do something about a better home for herself and the children. Listening to Mrs. Hargrove talk this morning had made her realize just how much her children thought about everything. She wondered how all of this temporariness was affecting them. They had lived hand-to-mouth all of their lives with their father. She wanted them to know they could trust her to take care of them and give them a normal life.

Barbara longed with all her heart to be deeply rooted in Dry Creek, but she had never asked herself if her children also felt like outsiders and wanted to belong. People seemed to have friendships that lasted a lifetime in this little town. Even people who grew up here and then moved away stayed connected. Barbara wanted that for herself and her children.

Barbara wondered what her children thought it would take to belong. She knew her signal was something as simple as being invited to pour coffee for those in the community. Her children might be longing for a real home to make them feel part of this small town. All of the other children here had regular houses. It was a normal expectation for a child.

She and the children might still have to wait for the people of Dry Creek to fully accept them as their own, but Barbara vowed she would do something now to let her children know it would happen soon.

It would probably be months before she could actually rent a place, and that included the old house Mr. Gossett's nephew was supposed to decide if he wanted to rent to her.

The house was across the street from where they were living now and down a little. Barbara could see its yard when she looked out the windows of the studio in front.

Often, during the day, she'd stop what she was doing and look across the street at that house. The fence around it was half falling down and the house itself had ceased being white a long time ago. Now, it looked mostly gray where the paint had been worn down by the winters around here. No grass grew in the yard. There were a few pine trees that had managed to survive around the house. Anything else that had once been planted had died, either because of the winter cold or the summer heat.

Barbara saw all of the house's shortcomings, but for her, that old place was a dream she wanted to come true. She could almost see what the place would look like if it had someone to care for it.

So far, Mrs. Hargrove hadn't received another letter saying the Gossetts had made the decision to rent the house to someone. And Mrs. Hargrove might not get such a letter for months.

Barbara decided her children couldn't wait much longer without hope that things would change. A sturdy table was a beginning, and she wanted to be able to give them that much now. It would signal that a change was going to happen.

Barbara knew she could afford a table if she sold the rings. She almost reached for the phone to ask Mrs. Hargrove to advise her on how to sell the three-ring set, but then she pulled back. She didn't want to have to run to Mrs. Hargrove for advice on everything.

There had to be a pawnshop in Miles City, Barbara reasoned. Maybe whoever ran it would give her a few hundred dollars for the rings. That was a quick and easy way to get money. She'd ask about catching a ride into town on Monday with Mrs. Hargrove. The older woman had said earlier that she was going to a dentist appointment then.

The whistle of the teakettle distracted Barbara, and before long she was holding a cup of hot tea. The steam from her cup warmed her face. The smell of cinnamon in the tea also made the room seem more welcoming. She wished she'd had tea steeping when she and the sheriff first got back here. She'd have to leave a pot steeping when he came back later to go to dinner. Mrs. Hargrove would probably like some tea while she watched the children anyway.

Forty-five minutes later, Barbara looked at herself in the old mirror that hung above the sink in the small bathroom next to the main room. The mirror had grown a little warped over the years, but it gave back a pretty accurate image even if it did make her face look yellow.

Barbara had washed and curled her hair until it flew around her face. She had brought out her makeup bag and put on a foundation cream and a little blush powder. She debated about putting on her eye liner and some green eye shadow before deciding that a little makeup couldn't define a dinner as a date. It was only natural that she wanted to look her best for the meal.

Barbara used the same logic as she pulled out one of the four dresses she owned. She'd picked the dress by elimination. Her oldest dress was a sleeveless cotton summer dress, and she didn't even consider that for tonight because it was too cold outside to wear it. Another dress was more of a navy suit, and Barbara had already decided she would keep that back for Sunday school and church tomorrow morning.

The third dress was that lavender bridesmaid's dress and Barbara knew she'd cause a huge amount of gossip if she wore that to dinner with the sheriff. She smiled to herself just thinking about it. Several of the younger couples in the area made it a habit to come to the café for the Saturday-night specials, so there'd be plenty of witnesses to her dinner with the sheriff. The story about her wearing a bridesmaid's dress to dinner with someone would last even longer than the story of her catching that bridal bouquet.

The remaining dress was her only choice, and that was the one Barbara was wearing. When she'd been married to Neal, this had been her "reconciliation dress." In the early days, when they'd had a fight, Neal would take her out someplace to dinner later and she would wear this dress. The dress was a deep violet that was so close to being black that it shimmered back and forth between the two colors, looking like one or the other depending on the way the light shone. The dress was fitted and long enough that it looked elegant. And it had a deep neckline that made it look even more as though it belonged in a supper club, especially when Barbara added a string of pearls around her neck.

Barbara always felt like a lady when she wore this dress.

She knew the dress was too elegant for her dinner with the sheriff, but Barbara had decided to wear it anyway. After the sheriff had gotten a good look at the room where she lived, it wouldn't hurt to try and impress him. She at least wanted him to know she had some nice clothes.

Barbara heard the car drive up to the steps leading into the outer studio room and come to a stop. She had left one of the overhead lights on in this room and she could see the shadows of two figures through the curtained window on the door. She listened for a knock.

The sheriff adjusted his tie. He hadn't fussed about what to wear some place in years. He knew he should probably have just put on a clean uniform and been done with it. That's what he would normally wear to a dinner business meeting. But he knew that this dinner wasn't about business; at least, it wasn't for him. So, he'd put on his one suit, the same black one he'd worn to the wedding and the same one he'd wear to church in the morning. At least he had a new white shirt to wear with it tonight. He had even borrowed Mrs. Hargrove's iron so he could press it.

"You look fine," Mrs. Hargrove said as she stepped up until she was even with him at the door. "Do you want me to knock?"

"No, I should knock." The sheriff rapped on the door with his knuckles. He wondered if Mrs. Hargrove knew how nervous he was.

"You're a handsome man, Carl Wall, and don't you be forgetting it," Mrs. Hargrove said staunchly as they listened to the footsteps coming toward the door.

"Thanks," the sheriff said, resisting the urge to smooth down his hair. He knew Mrs. Hargrove was just being supportive, but he did appreciate her telling him he looked fine. And everything would go fine, too; he just needed to take a deep breath and relax. The sheriff got his breath out, but he never got it back in again.

The door opened instead and he saw a movie star. Or one of those fancy magazine models. Whoever it was, she was dressed to go somewhere on the arm of a millionaire instead of a poor man who was going to pass out any minute now if he didn't take a deep breath.

The sheriff gulped.

Mrs. Hargrove slapped him on the back at the same time as she said hello to Barbara.

"Is he okay?" Barbara asked Mrs. Hargrove.

"More than okay," the older woman said. "I think he's going to do just fine."

The sheriff breathed again. At least, he thought he must be breathing, because he hadn't passed out.

"I'll just go on back to where the children are," Mrs. Hargrove said as she walked through the doorway and headed toward the back room. "You two have fun now."

The sheriff noticed that that thought seemed to alarm Barbara.

"We're going to work on a slogan," Barbara turned to say the older woman.

Mrs. Hargrove didn't even break her stride

as she walked across the floor toward the back room. "You'll come up with a good one, too."

Mrs. Hargrove entered the back room, and the sheriff heard the excited shrieks of the children.

"I see they woke up," he said, wishing for the tenth time today that he'd been born with the gift of gab. He'd never seen the use of chitchat before tonight. But now he was coming to appreciate the skill of making small talk, even though he didn't have any of it.

Barbara nodded. "I fed them a sandwich earlier."

The sheriff nodded. "Do you need to do anything else before we go? Because I can wait if you need. That's no problem."

The sheriff paused for breath. He sure wondered what Pete Denning would say to a woman in this same situation. "You did something different with your hair. It's nice." The sheriff wondered if that was adequate. "Real nice."

Barbara smiled as she lifted one of her hands to her hair. "Thanks. And I guess I'm ready. Just let me go get my shawl. It looks cold outside."

The sheriff nodded. "It is a little chilly."

The sheriff watched Barbara walk across the floor to the doorway of the back room. He hoped he could catch his breath while she was back there. He didn't want to give the impression that he couldn't walk a few steps without being winded. Especially now, because he planned to offer his arm to Barbara for the walk down the street to the café. He'd decided when he put the suit on earlier that it would be the proper thing to do.

If he didn't get his wind back though, she might think he was offering his arm so that she could steady him. That wasn't the impression he wanted to give. Not at all. He took another deep breath. This one sat easier inside. Mrs. Hargrove was right. He'd do fine.

Chapter Eleven

Barbara hadn't stepped completely through the door into the café before she knew something was wrong. She'd walked into this same café hundreds of times in the past five months, and she'd never seen it look like this.

Usually on Saturday evenings, Linda added a candle to each table. But she also had fluorescent tube lighting in the ceiling that streamed down and gave everything a homey appearance. The candles were only an accent. No one actually ate by candlelight.

The Dry Creek Café wasn't a romantic place. It had a black-and-white-checked linoleum floor, and even with the white tablecloths Linda used on Saturday nights, it looked like a place where one would go to order a hamburger with friends instead of a gourmet meal with a date. In fact, the usual Saturday-night specials were bacon cheeseburgers and T-bone steaks.

But tonight was different. The lighting was so low no one could see the person in front of them, let alone the color of the floor at their feet. Soft instrumental music was playing on the stereo Linda kept in the kitchen. Even Linda herself was transformed. Instead of wearing her usual T-shirt and jeans, she was wearing a black dress with a white collar and a white bib apron. Linda's hair was drawn back into a bun and clipped with a gold barrette.

"Isn't anyone else having dinner?" Barbara whispered when she and the sheriff walked past Linda. Usually, the café had a half dozen people in it at this hour. In the past month or so, Linda had even been talking about hiring extra help. Saturday was the big night for people in Dry Creek to go out to dinner. The place shouldn't be empty.

"The Redferns were in earlier and ate," Linda said calmly as she closed the door behind

Barbara and the sheriff. "Oh, and the Curtis family were here, too. And the Martins."

"But it's not even dinnertime yet, and they're all finished," Barbara said. She couldn't believe it. "What about the Elktons? They always come in around this time on Saturday night. They're like clockwork."

"They ordered takeout tonight. I just gave them their bag not five minutes ago."

"Takeout? No one ever orders takeout here."

Linda shrugged and gestured for Barbara and the sheriff to sit at the one table that had been moved to the center of the room. It was clearly a table for two, its size small enough for close conversation. Usually, large group tables sat in the middle of the café floor. Barbara knew the smaller table had been placed there especially for her and the sheriff. Someone had even stuck a long red rose in a silver vase and put it in the center of the table. For good measure, there was a doily under the vase.

"My best table," Linda said as she pulled back one of the straight-back chairs.

The sheriff stayed standing until Barbara sat down and then he moved closer to settle her chair under the table.

When the sheriff finished pushing in her chair, he went back and sat in the other chair.

"Our specials tonight are garlic-roasted pork loin or grilled Atlantic salmon. Both are served with cream of asparagus soup and a nice rice pilaf," Linda announced.

"Cream of asparagus soup," Barbara repeated. What had happened to the chili burgers and tuna melts? Even the steaks Linda offered on Saturday nights were usually served with fries. People in Dry Creek didn't eat much rice pilaf. She was sure they didn't eat asparagus soup. "That sounds good."

"Which would you like?" the sheriff asked.

"I'll take the salmon," Barbara answered.

"Make that two," the sheriff said.

Linda nodded and walked back to the kitchen area.

Barbara waited until she and the sheriff were alone before she whispered, "Did you make some kind of special reservations for dinner tonight?"

The sheriff shook his head. "I didn't make any reservations at all—no one has ever needed reservations here before. I did mention to Mrs. Hargrove what time we were planning to eat, but that was only because she needed to know so she could watch the children."

"I'd guess that more people than Mrs. Hargrove know that we're having dinner here tonight at six-thirty," Barbara said.

The sheriff nodded. "I'm glad I wore my suit." He looked at Barbara and smiled. "I would hate to waste all of this on my uniform. Linda's gone to a lot of work."

"Pork loin and salmon? I guess we should feel honored," Barbara said.

Barbara knew there was a general misunderstanding being spread around Dry Creek. No one else had private dining in the café. Either she or the sheriff had the measles, or there was some other reason they were being left alone tonight.

"They think we're on a date," Barbara stated the obvious.

"Maybe we are," the sheriff said.

"I don't think—"

"We're both dressed up and eating together by candlelight at a table with a fresh rose on it," the sheriff declared. "And people are worried about our privacy. Oh, yeah, we're on a date."

"Well, maybe—but it's a business date. To figure out a campaign slogan."

The sheriff shrugged. "We can do that, too. It shouldn't take long. How about Vote for the Sheriff?"

"You at least need to have your name with it," Barbara protested. "People might vote for your competition instead if you're not clear."

"I don't have any competition. Besides, people always call me the sheriff. Mrs. Hargrove is the only one who uses my name."

"Oh." Barbara blinked. That didn't seem quite right to her somehow. "Everyone should have a name that people use."

"Folks around here just know me as the sheriff."

Barbara smiled. "But what if you weren't the sheriff, what then?"

The sheriff looked at her as though she'd suggested the unthinkable. "I've been the sheriff here for fifteen years—ever since I was twenty-one."

A loud noise interrupted them. It sounded as if several pots and pans had fallen on the floor in the kitchen. Barbara's suspicions were confirmed when she saw Linda poke her head out of the kitchen door. Linda's black dress was still neat, but her hair looked like she'd been through a whirlwind. The bun was gone and strands of dark hair fluttered around her face.

"I'm sorry for the racket," Linda said, a little breathlessly. "I'll have your soup out in a minute. I just need to whip up some more—if I can find some more asparagus back there. I thought I bought more."

"Don't worry about the soup," the sheriff said.

"But we wanted the dinner to be special for you," Linda fretted. "Especially since it's your first date and all."

The sheriff put his hand over the one Barbara had on the table as though to stop the words he knew were ready to come out of her mouth. She supposed he was right. No one believed her when she said it wasn't a date anyway.

"We're doing just fine here," the sheriff said.

Barbara nodded. "We'd be fine with hamburgers and fries too, if that's easier for you."

"You would?" Linda said. She looked relieved.

"I've always liked the hamburgers here," the sheriff said. "Some of the best in the state—especially the ones with the pepper jack cheese on them."

Barbara wondered how long the sheriff expected to keep his hand over hers. He'd probably forgotten that he even had it there, and she knew he had only put it there as a request that she be silent, but she still thought he should move it. It was causing her to feel, well, warm for one thing. Plus, it was also causing her to remember that kiss the sheriff had given her when she was in the hospital. He'd never even mentioned it since. The man must make a habit of making gestures that he never acknowledged.

"You're a flirt," Barbara said when Linda had gone back into the kitchen. The sheriff's hand still cradled hers.

"What?" The sheriff seemed astonished.

Barbara nodded. "You could move your hand. I got your message. But you just leave it there like you don't even know that it's there. Conveniently forgotten. It's just like that kiss you gave me in the hospital. You do it and then you don't even bother to acknowledge it."

"I—" The sheriff cleared his throat.

Barbara nodded again for emphasis. "I suppose you're worried that I'll mistake them for something they are not, so you don't even mention them. But it's only polite to at least acknowledge that something happened—"

"I—" The sheriff looked a little short of breath again.

Maybe that's why he still hadn't moved his hand.

"You should know that I am not foolish enough to read anything into a kiss—no matter how good it was—or to make something over a little hand-holding, even if it is in public," Barbara stated.

The sheriff's hand moved, only not in the direction Barbara had anticipated. Instead of moving away, his hand moved around until he had hers firmly in his grasp. "You thought the kiss was good, huh?"

The sheriff didn't look at all as though he had trouble breathing now. He even grinned.

Barbara wondered if she was the one who needed some air. "You were very good to me when I was in the hospital—I'm grateful for that."

Barbara remembered how close she'd felt to the sheriff then. She'd told him all her secrets. She'd never told Neal things like that, not even in the early days when she'd still loved him. The sheriff had heard all her dreams and her fears. She'd thought later that it was the pain medication that had loosened her tongue. She usually didn't trust men with her inner thoughts. But maybe it had been something more. It was odd that sitting across the table from him now in this darkened café, she was starting to feel close again.

"I don't need your gratitude," the sheriff said as he moved his hand away. His grin was gone. "It's my job to help people."

Barbara wondered when it had gotten so cold in the room. Then someone opened the outside door and enough wind blew in to lower the temperature even more.

"Who turned the lights off?" a man's voice said from where he stood by the open door.

The room was so dark that it was hard to see the man clearly. Barbara thought she recognized Pete Denning, but she wasn't sure until she saw the reflection from that gold-plated belt buckle of his.

"We're closed," Linda said as she walked out from the kitchen and into the main café area.

"How can you be closed when they're here?" Pete said as he took a step into the café. "Besides, they're the ones I wanted to see."

"Is there trouble somewhere?" the sheriff asked, as he began to rise from the table.

"Probably," Pete said as he walked over to their table. "But I'm not here about trouble. I'm here to do my civic duty."

The sheriff sat back down and asked cautiously, "What civic duty would that be?"

"You never do your civic duty, Peter Denning, and don't you pretend otherwise," Linda said as she walked further into the room. She had a spatula in one hand and she waved it around for emphasis. "Why, you don't even vote."

"I voted last election," Pete protested.

Barbara thought he sounded a little self-righteous.

Linda snorted. "I heard. You voted for Santa Claus. All the slots—even the school board members."

Pete grinned. "Well, I figure Santa's been good to me, and it's the least I can do for him. The old man seems to have an image problem around here."

"That's because he's not a real person," Linda said as she pointed at Pete with the spatula. "No one votes for someone who isn't real."

Pete grinned even wider. "Half of the politicians in the world aren't real either. They're just images created by their public relations staff. At least Santa Claus is around from year to year and doesn't take a dive on the voters."

"Well, I don't care who you vote for, you just can't do it tonight. Not here. We have an exclusive party here." Linda said as she marched up to Pete and took his elbow in her hand so that he had to rise up from the chair he'd pulled close to the table. "If you drive around to the alley in back, I can give you a take-out hamburger through the back window."

"Like a drive-in?" Pete said in amazement. He stopped walking. "Since when do you do a drive-in business?"

"Since we have a date in the front dining room—" Linda ground out the words,

Barbara didn't even think about protesting. She was having too much fun watching Linda and Pete grimace at each other. She was going to have to ask Linda if Pete was the man who had left her broken-hearted some years ago. There certainly seemed to be something between the two of them. Maybe it wasn't as hopeless as Linda thought.

"They aren't on a date," Pete said as he shook his arm free from Linda's hand. "It's a business meeting to set up a slogan for the sheriff's political campaign. Barbara told me that herself."

Pete looked at Barbara, and she felt she had to nod in confirmation even though by now she was confused as to what this evening was.

"It's both a date and a campaign meeting," the sheriff finally said as he ran his finger under his collar and loosened his tie. "The one thing it sure isn't, however, is dinner." The sheriff smiled toward Linda before turning to Pete. "Not that it won't be dinner just as soon as you let the cook get back to her cooking."

"Well, I guess I could settle for a hamburger to go," Pete said grudgingly. "I'm just trying to figure out what's what around here."

Barbara could sympathize with the ranch hand.

"I'll throw in a batch of fries if you wait out back," Linda offered Pete as she gestured toward the door.

Pete lifted an eyebrow, but he did begin to walk toward the door. "With some of that barbecue sauce on the side?"

"I know how you like your fries," Linda said.

Barbara couldn't help but notice that the ranch hand turned around to watch Linda as she walked back into the kitchen. And when he did, he had a vulnerable look on his face that made Barbara wonder.

"Well, that was interesting," Barbara said when Pete finally left the café. "How long ago was it that he and Linda dated?"

"Pete and Linda?" the sheriff asked in surprise. "Why there's nothing between the two of them. Linda's been waiting for that boyfriend of hers, Jazz, to give up on that band of his and come home. She's been waiting a good three years now. They started this café together before he left Dry Creek to try and become a rock star. What a waste of a man's future."

"Three years is a long time to wait for someone," Barbara said slowly. She could already smell the hamburgers cooking on the grill in back. She also heard the sound of a pickup driving around behind the café.

"How long are you planning to wait?" the sheriff said quietly. "Before you marry again, that is."

"Oh." Barbara flushed. "I'm not going to marry again."

The sheriff didn't say anything.

"I'm just not very good at it," Barbara finally confessed, partly because she felt uncomfortable not giving any reason at all. Plus, there was nothing else to fill the silence.

The sheriff shook his head. "I don't believe it. Now me, I'm the one who wouldn't know how to go about this family business. But you? You have it down pat already."

Maybe it was the fact that the café was still dark and she only saw flashes of the sheriff's face. It was like being in a confessional. Whatever it was, Barbara went ahead and told him everything. "It's not about family life. I can do that. It's just that I'm not any good at picking men. You know, like some women aren't any good at picking watermelons. I don't seem to do very well with picking men. I doubt Neal ever loved me, not even at first when I thought he did. I should have known better."

They sat in silence for a moment.

"I figure a woman can learn to pick out a good watermelon," the sheriff finally said. "And, if she can't, she gets a neighbor to help her pick one out."

Barbara smiled at that. "I don't know of too many neighbors who want to pick out a husband for someone."

The sheriff snorted. "You could've fooled me on that one. It seems everyone around here has an opinion on who should marry who."

Barbara frowned. Now that she thought about it, that was true. "Especially who should marry me."

She remembered the night of the wedding reception when Charley had offered his nephew and Jacob had offered himself.

"But it's not the same," Barbara said. "No one should pick out a partner for someone else. It should be something special that just happens between the two people."

"I wouldn't know about that," the sheriff said.

Love was a whole lot different than picking out a watermelon, Barbara thought. Love made a woman lose the sense she was born with. Picking out a ripe piece of fruit never did that.

She didn't get a chance to tell the sheriff that though, because the door to the kitchen opened and Linda came out with a small plastic basket in her hands. "I thought I'd bring you some fries to get you started. Your hamburgers will be out in a minute. What kind of cheese do you want?"

"I'll stick with the pepper jack," the sheriff said.

"I'll have mine plain," Barbara said. "With lots of catsup."

"And some mustard for me," the sheriff added.

Linda set the basket of fries down on the table and went back into the kitchen.

Barbara and the sheriff were silent for a minute.

"I'm not planning to get married again

anyway," Barbara finally said. She thought she should tell him that. After all, he had been kind enough to understand her watermelon theory.

The sheriff nodded as he picked up the basket. "You've made your feeling on that subject clear. Want some fries?"

Barbara reached into the basket and pulled out a hot French fry. "I think Linda should get married though. I can't help thinking about Pete and her."

The sheriff grinned. "See what I mean about picking out watermelons for your neighbors? Everybody wants to do it."

"Who would you pick?"

"For you?" the sheriff said. His grin was gone and he looked serious.

Barbara shook her head. "No, for Linda."

"I'd pick Pete," the sheriff said promptly. "Just to keep him away from you."

"That's not a very good reason."

"It is to me," the sheriff said with a nod. "He's not good enough for you. Not by a long shot. You need to marry a man with—" the sheriff seemed at a momentary loss for words "—well, with lots of money, I guess."

Barbara gasped. "I'd never marry a man for his money."

"Of course, you wouldn't," the sheriff agreed and wiggled his eyebrows. "That's why you need to let a neighbor like me do the picking for you."

Barbara laughed. She had forgotten about the sheriff's eyebrows. He'd told some of the best stories when she was in the hospital and, as often as not, they'd ended with that wiggle of his eyebrows. She didn't even pay any attention to the sounds of the kitchen door opening.

When the sheriff saw she was laughing, he wiggled his ears, too. And then his nose.

"You need to read a bedtime story to the children some night," she said when she got her breath back from laughing. "You'd do a great three little pigs."

Barbara gradually became aware that Linda was walking toward them.

"I brought your hamburgers," Linda said cautiously as she sat two platters down on the table. "I'll be back with the catsup and mustard."

Barbara wiped a tear away that she'd

gotten from laughing. "Thank you, we're really not crazy. We're just—"

Linda held up her hand. "You don't need to explain. Tonight I'm an anonymous waitress. Your date is private."

"Well, it's not so much a date as it is—" Barbara stopped to think a minute. "Well, really, it's just two old friends having dinner together."

The sheriff nodded. "I can live with that. As long as it's not just business."

Linda smiled and turned her back to walk toward the kitchen. "There'll be blueberry pie for dessert if you want some."

"Blueberry is my favorite," the sheriff said. "We'll sit here a bit after we eat our hamburgers and have some."

"And we do need to think of a slogan for you," Barbara said.

"We've got time," the sheriff said. "I'm not fussy and I don't mind lingering over dessert."

Barbara felt the sheriff's hand cover the hand she had on the table again and give it a squeeze before letting it go.

"Right now you're probably hungry for these hamburgers though," the sheriff said as he unfolded the cloth napkin by his plate and put it on his lap.

Barbara couldn't remember when she'd tasted a better hamburger.

"Uhmmm, that's good," the sheriff said as he took a bite of his own hamburger.

Barbara smiled. She liked watching the sheriff enjoy his meal. She liked the way the evening had slipped into friendship as well. She took another bite of her hamburger.

After a minute, Barbara sat her hamburger down on the plate. "Now isn't this better than being on a date? Just two friends eating together. No pressure. No—you know—"

The sheriff lifted his eyebrow as he put down his own hamburger. "'No—you know'? What's that?"

Barbara shrugged. "Holding hands. Kissing. That sort of thing."

The sheriff smiled. "Oh, I intend for there to be kissing."

"But—"

"It wouldn't be fair to have Linda go to all this work for us and us not even to kiss after," the sheriff said. "It might discourage her from doing this sort of thing for others."

Barbara knew she should protest. But somehow she didn't really want to argue about it. It seemed churlish to argue when the stereo in the kitchen was playing old love songs now. She could afford to kiss the man again. In fact, she'd begun to wonder what it would be like to kiss the sheriff again now that she was free of pain and not sedated at all. She'd probably find out that a kiss now wasn't the same as the one had been back then anyway. It would actually be good for her to kiss the sheriff. It'd be an experiment of sorts.

If the sheriff had expected an argument, he didn't say. He just kept eating his hamburger as though everything were normal. But Barbara knew that things were far from normal. For one thing, the temperature in the café had shot up as though someone had turned the furnace on. For another, the hamburger that had tasted so good a moment ago now tasted like sawdust.

Barbara had finished her hamburger before she convinced herself that the sheriff had been teasing her about the kiss. He must have been teasing, because he looked as if he'd completely forgotten about any kiss. Between bites, he kept humming along with the tunes on the stereo. When he did talk, it was about the weather. A man didn't do that if he had kissing on his mind. Yes, he must have been just teasing her.

Barbara and the sheriff had both finished their hamburgers and folded their napkins when Barbara realized how wrong she had been. The sheriff hadn't forgotten and he hadn't been teasing.

The sheriff stood up and offered his hand to Barbara. "Would you like to take a stroll before dessert?"

Barbara didn't even have to answer him; he just put her hand in the curve of his elbow and escorted her out of the café and onto the front steps. Together they stepped down onto the ground.

"Let's step out a few feet," the sheriff said as he led her away from the building. "We can see the stars better then."

On the walk over to the café, Barbara hadn't paid any attention to the sky. Now she was surprised anyone could walk beneath it and not notice the spattering of jewels up there.

"The clouds left at least," the sheriff said as he looked up. "I was hoping they would."

So that's why he was wondering about the weather during dinner, Barbara realized. He wanted to be sure they could see the stars.

"It's beautiful," Barbara said softly.

They were silent for a moment, just looking upward.

"I guess this makes it a date officially," Barbara said with a little laugh. "We're out looking at the moon and the stars."

"No, that doesn't make it official. This does."

Barbara felt the sheriff turn toward her and she lifted her face to his. She told herself it was not a real kiss. It was just a kiss to knock the memory of that other kiss out of her mind.

The next thought she had was that looking at the sky wasn't the only way to see stars. She felt the sheriff's kiss all the way down to her stomach. Or was it her toes?

"Oh, my." Barbara breathed when she could.

The sheriff took his own deep breath. "—dear."

Barbara looked up in panic. The sheriff was going too fast.

The sheriff looked at her for a moment before smiling a little ruefully. "That's the way it all goes. It's 'oh, my dear.'"

"Oh," Barbara said in relief. "That's right."

Trust the sheriff to think about things like completing a phrase at a time like this, Barbara thought to herself as they walked back into the café. But it was good that one of them was thinking of something sensible. She didn't quite seem able to at this time.

Chapter Twelve

It seemed like a long walk to Sunday school the next morning even though the church was only two doors down and across the street from the place where Barbara and the children lived. Barbara could see that the children were much more excited about going there than she was.

"They have a birthday bank," Bobby had confided to her this morning over a breakfast of toast and cereal. "On your birthday, you get to go up and put a penny in the bank for every year old you are. Then they sing Happy Birthday to you and give you a pencil."

Barbara had no idea that Bobby knew so much about what happened in the Sunday school at the Dry Creek Church. The other kids had obviously told him all about it.

"And they sing songs," Amanda had added solemnly as she carefully poured milk on her second bowl of cereal. "But nobody has to sing all by themselves so it's not scary."

"I'm sure none of it will be scary," Barbara had told the children.

And, even now that they were walking toward the church on this fine spring morning, she was sure that what she had said was true for the children. She, on the other hand, had every right to be terrified about going to Sunday school.

People expected adults to have at least a nodding acquaintance with what went on in a church. Barbara didn't. She knew about the Golden Rule and the Lord's Prayer, but she didn't know anything about what actually went on in a church. She didn't know if you bowed to the minister or stood when the choir sang. She knew the Christmas story, but that's all she knew about the Bible.

Yet, even though she had told Mrs. Hargrove that she didn't know anything, the older woman had still wanted her to help with her first- and second-grade Sunday-school class. Amanda and Bobby would both normally be in that class, so she had agreed. She didn't make her children go to the dentist alone; she wouldn't make them go to Sunday school alone either.

Besides, Barbara didn't plan on making Sunday school a habit, so she didn't suppose it mattered what class any of them attended. At least Mrs. Hargrove had a class of younger children instead of junior-high kids. Barbara hoped the class would be easy.

Barbara adjusted the jacket of her suit and then took both of her children's hands in hers before she started up the steps to the church. Even though they'd never had a steady home, she had taken the children to the dentist at least once a year. It was just one of those things a parent had to do for their child. Church was probably like that, too. They could do this, she told herself.

Fifteen minutes later, Barbara decided she was wrong. She, for one, couldn't do this. She should have known better. They didn't even have Novocain.

It had been easy enough to get directions

to the room where Mrs. Hargrove held her Sunday-school class and the stairs down to the basement were clearly marked. The basement had been painted bright colors and there were high windows along all of the walls. The basement was marked off into several areas for different Sunday-school classes and each area had a long kid-sized table with a dozen chairs around it. Mrs. Hargrove had a chalkboard in her area with her name on it so Barbara would have known which space belonged to the older woman's class even if Mrs. Hargrove hadn't been there.

Finding the right place seemed to go pretty well, Barbara thought. After that though, things stopped being easy.

Five minutes after Barbara and the children settled into chairs around the table, Mrs. Hargrove led the children in a game called a sword drill. The older woman gave Bibles to both Bobby and Amanda so they could play with the other children.

Barbara was glad that Mrs. Hargrove hadn't offered her a Bible. She didn't know where anything was located in the Bible, and it was quickly obvious that this was the skill required to solve puzzles in the game. Mrs. Hargrove called out a man's name with a number behind it—like John 3:16—and the children tried to be the first to find where those words were written in their Bibles. Barbara was dumbfounded that the little kids could find things so quickly. She wouldn't have even known that the children weren't using the full Bible if Mrs. Hargrove hadn't told her.

Fortunately, the sword drill didn't last long and then it was time for the sheriff to tell the story. Correction, Barbara reminded herself, it was time for Carl Wall to tell the story. She had decided some time during the night that she was Carl's friend and friends called each other by their name and not their job title.

By the look on Carl's face, he could use a friend about now, so Barbara nodded encouragingly to him as he stood up. He'd been sitting in a folding chair in the back corner of the room until he stood. Barbara thought he looked a little uneasy until one of the boys rolled a piece of paper into a wad the size of a marble and threw it at the girl across the table from him.

Carl straightened right up then. "That's not allowed in here."

* * *

The sheriff saw the look of panic on the boy's face and glanced at Mrs. Hargrove. He didn't want the older woman to have a heart attack because he'd frightened one of her precious students. Besides, the boy was probably only six years old, and right now he was stiffer than some men had been when he'd called out, "Drop it."

The sheriff thought the boy was a Campbell—Sam or Danny or something like that. He knew the boy's father was Frank Campbell. Frank worked for a gas station between here and Miles City.

"No spit wads," the sheriff said in what he hoped was friendlier voice than he'd used initially. To make sure he was nice enough, he added a smile. "We're here to learn, not throw things at each other."

At least that's why the kids were here, the sheriff told himself. He was here because he'd bartered his Sunday morning in exchange for his Saturday night and, as uncomfortable as he was now, he still thought he'd gotten the better of the deal.

"She started it first," the boy said with an

indignant protest. "She kicked me under the table."

The sheriff looked at the girl that the Campbell boy was scowling at and, sure enough, she wouldn't meet the sheriff's eyes. The boy's trouble with women was starting early. The sheriff knew the girl's name. It was Suzy Holmquist. The family lived out by the Elkton place.

"Well, there's better ways to handle things," the sheriff finally told the boy.

"Are you going to arrest me?" the boy asked, looking defiantly up at the sheriff. "Bobby told me you might arrest him if he didn't do his homework."

Where did the kids come up with these ideas? the sheriff wondered. "I'm not arresting anybody today."

"Not even if a bad man shows up?" Suzy asked, finally deciding it was okay to look the sheriff in the eye. "You'd have to arrest a bad man. You're the sheriff. It's your job to protect everyone in Dry Creek."

"I'm off on Sundays," the sheriff said.

"Oh." Suzy looked surprised. "Well, who protects us on Sundays?"

The sheriff looked over at Mrs. Hargrove. He was out of his league with these kids, and he had the good sense to know it. "You're sure you don't want a new roof instead?"

Mrs. Hargrove smiled as she shook her head. She did, however, stand up, which to the sheriff's dismay seemed to make the children pay a little more attention to what was going on. He doubted anyone kicked anyone else under the table while Mrs. Hargrove was on duty.

"Suzy is asking a good question, class," Mrs. Hargrove said. "Who protects us if the sheriff isn't around?"

There was a moment of silence.

"My dog," one boy said hesitantly. "He's good at scaring people away."

Mrs. Hargrove nodded. "Is there anyone else who is even more powerful than your dog?"

"She means God," a redheaded girl said. "He's around to help us out if we meet up with trouble."

There was another moment of silence.

"God would have a hard time beating up a bad guy," another boy said. "I'd rather have the sheriff working on Sundays."

The sheriff knew he shouldn't let that make him feel good, but it did. Though, at least he had the sense to know that it wasn't what Mrs. Hargrove wanted to hear.

"Can the sheriff protect you from twenty lions even if he doesn't have a gun?" Mrs. Hargrove asked the class.

The sheriff was gratified to see that the children seemed to be debating the question instead of just saying no.

"Does he have pepper spray?" Suzy finally asked.

Mrs. Hargrove shook her head. "He has absolutely nothing."

Several of the children shook their heads.

"The sheriff is going to tell you what happened to a man who had to face more than twenty lions and didn't have a gun or pepper spray or anything," Mrs. Hargrove said and then paused. "Well, he did have one secret weapon. Listen to the story and see what it was."

The sheriff had to admit that Mrs. Hargrove did know how to get the attention of these kids. They were all caught up in the story of Daniel in the lion's den even though

the sheriff just read it to them from the book
Mrs. Hargrove had given him. He showed
them the pictures from time to time, but the
children seemed content just to listen to the
words being read.

"And so, what was the man's secret
weapon?" Mrs. Hargrove asked when the
story was finished.

"God," the children answered together.

"And what did he do when he was in trouble?"

"He asked God to help him," Suzy said.

Mrs. Hargrove nodded. "That's what we do
when we pray. We ask God to help us. And then
we trust Him to do what He has promised."

Barbara felt as if she'd run a marathon.
She'd watched the expressions on the faces
of Amanda and Bobby as they listened to the
story, and she could see the longing in each
of them. She was clearly not all that her
children needed to feel safe and protected. If
she were, they wouldn't be looking so hungry
for more words to the story.

She had to admit she felt a certain wist-
fulness herself. She would sleep better at

night if she believed someone was watching out for her, listening to her prayers or cries. She supposed though that one had to have the trust of a child to believe such a thing. She'd long since given up on being that trusting of anyone.

"Thank you, Carl," Mrs. Hargrove said as the sheriff went back to the chair he had sat in earlier.

Somewhere a bell rang.

"That leaves us five minutes," Mrs. Hargrove said. "Just enough time to say a few prayers. Who wants to go first?"

Barbara watched her children bow their heads along with the other children. One of the boys prayed that his brother would get over the flu. A girl prayed for the children in Africa.

And then Barbara's heart stopped because her daughter prayed. Amanda's voice was clear and steady as she made her request. "Dear God, my mommy wants a house for us to live in."

"Amen," Mrs. Hargrove said just as she'd said at the end of each child's prayer.

Barbara just sat in her seat until the children finished praying and scrambled out of their seats to go upstairs. Before long, Amanda and Bobby were the only children left around the table.

"Thank you," Mrs. Hargrove said as she looked from Barbara to the sheriff. "You've been a blessing."

"Carl told a good story, didn't he?" Barbara said.

The sheriff looked surprised. "No one except Mrs. Hargrove calls me Carl."

"They do now," Mrs. Hargrove said with an approving nod at Barbara. "And it's about time."

Barbara liked seeing someone as flustered as she felt. Both she and Carl were in foreign territory here. Neither one of them had even intended to come to church. Mrs. Hargrove had just been so compelling. "We forgot to take some pictures."

Barbara had a disposable camera in her purse and she had been all set to take a few shots.

"We can try again next Sunday," Mrs. Hargrove said serenely.

"Next Sunday?" Carl said with a gulp. "The deal was for *this* Sunday."

Mrs. Hargrove smiled slightly. "I understand you both had a good time last night. I thought you might want to repeat the deal next weekend."

"Does everybody know about our d—" Barbara stopped herself from saying *date*. "About our dinner?"

"Oh, I expect so, dear," Mrs. Hargrove said, just as though it weren't anything unusual.

Carl grunted. "Maybe next Saturday we should drive into Miles City."

Barbara smiled. So there was going to be a next Saturday.

"There's a coffee time before church," Mrs. Hargrove said as she picked up her books. "Next to the kitchen in the area at the top of the stairs."

"Do you need anyone to pour the coffee?" Barbara asked. It was starting to be a rather nice day. It wouldn't hurt to ask.

"Oh, no, dear," Mrs. Hargrove said as she started walking toward the stairs that led up to the main part of the church. "We couldn't ask you to do that. You're a guest."

"Oh," Barbara said.

"They have cookies, too," Bobby said as he and Amanda walked over to Barbara. "Some guys told me. He said to take the ones that have chocolate chips in them."

Barbara could see her children would want to come to Sunday school again.

"Well, I guess we wouldn't want to miss out on the cookies," the sheriff said as he put his hand on Bobby's shoulder and the two of them started walking toward the stairs.

Barbara put her hand on Amanda's shoulder and started walking too. She supposed they would all sit together during church. She almost hoped so. Her worry about doing the wrong thing in church would be easier with someone beside her who could arrest people for harassment if things went bad.

Chapter Thirteen

Floyd Spencer looked at the church building and swore. He hadn't planned to drive back to Dry Creek this morning. He'd seen that the cake was delivered yesterday, and he thought that would be enough for the time being.

But last night someone had come into his house while he was sleeping and left a note taped to his bathroom mirror. The note said he had three more days. There was no signature to the note, but he knew who it was from. Harlow Smith was letting him know that the cake wasn't enough.

Floyd didn't know what to do. The door to his house had been double-locked. The windows had been locked, too. Whoever had come inside hadn't even had to break into his house, and he'd even changed the locks a few weeks ago. Someone had picked the lock. That was the only explanation. And if Harlow had someone working for him who could pick locks, Floyd wasn't safe anywhere.

Floyd knew it was probably foolish of him to come to Dry Creek. He'd spent the past hour hiding behind those pine trees in back of the deserted house. He didn't want anyone to see him. But he was a desperate man. If he could find a way to take that boy of Neal's as a hostage, that's what he was going to do. He'd already nosed around that place where Neal's wife and the kids stayed, but they weren't there this morning. It looked like the only place they could be was in that church there.

He'd hoped to catch the boy alone, but it didn't look like that was going to happen today.

Floyd patted his pocket. He needed one of those antacid pills. He'd bought another packet this morning at the same grocery store next to the motel where he stayed in Miles City. At this rate, he'd spend all of the money he'd gotten from the robbery on gas driving out to Dry Creek and on antacid pills to keep his stomach settled down.

Chapter Fourteen

The next morning, for the first time in fifteen years, the sheriff stood in front of his bedroom mirror and debated about whether or not to put on his uniform. Of course, he knew he had to put it on. Monday was a working day for him, and people needed to know that he was on duty.

It was just this business of Barbara calling him Carl that made him feel unsettled inside. He'd always liked people calling him Sheriff instead of Carl. It said who he was, and that was enough. People needed a sheriff.

It should be enough for a man, shouldn't it? The sheriff shook his head. He wished he knew. It had certainly been enough for him for all these years.

He'd never had a family and he'd never expected to have any friends. He didn't need to be more than the sheriff to anyone. Or did he?

He wasn't sure what had changed things for him. Maybe it was Barbara using his first name all morning yesterday or maybe it was sitting with her and her two children during church. Whatever it was, he found himself having dreams of something he'd never known—a family. At least, he thought it was dreams of having a family. He didn't even know what a family felt like. He'd never come close to anything like it in all those places where he'd lived growing up. He hadn't even missed it. Everyone had limitations. He'd been content with his life. Until now.

The sheriff reached for his shirt and started putting it on.

Church had been a surprising thing for him, too. He'd never thought someone like him belonged in a place like that. Church was mostly for families and children.

He had always been more comfortable with the ranch hands, his boots hitched up on a corral when the rodeo hit Miles City. He hadn't thought he would like sitting in church, but he had. People came up and shook his hand after the whole thing was over and he knew he was welcome. The church at Dry Creek didn't have any of the fancy frills he'd feared, either. The building was a place where people could just be themselves.

The sheriff reached for his pants.

He'd been able to follow the talk Matthew Curtis had given, the sheriff thought with satisfaction. It was mostly about a person trusting God when they were in trouble. The sheriff had no problem with people doing that. He knew he couldn't be everywhere. It was good for people to ask God for help sometimes, too.

Of course, the sheriff hoped no one was foolish enough to ask God for help when they really needed a sheriff instead. After all, a lawman carried a gun.

The sheriff reached for his belt that looped onto his gun holster.

Yes, the sheriff told himself, he needed to be ready to do his job. Today was a day just like any other work day.

When he had finished dressing, the sheriff walked over to his dresser and opened the top drawer. Somewhere in there he had a brass name badge that he'd been issued with his uniform years ago. He shoved aside some socks and found it. It wouldn't hurt to wear the badge, he told himself as he pinned it on to his shirt—just in case other people wanted to call him by name, too.

Barbara started baking early so she'd get the donuts and the pies ready this morning before nine. It was a fairly light day for bakery orders; Monday always was, probably because people ordered so much for Saturday that by Monday they were thinking they needed to eat a little more fruit instead of baked goods.

She was fine with having a quick morning today though because Mrs. Hargrove had happily agreed to take her into Miles City at ten o'clock when she went for her dental appointment. The children had both caught the school bus at seven-thirty and it was a good day for Barbara to go to Miles City. Mrs. Hargrove had even offered Barbara the use of her car while she was in the dental office so that Barbara could do her errands.

Barbara was determined to find a pawnshop in Miles City so she could ask about selling the ring set she had. Ever since Amanda had voiced her prayer for a house, Barbara had been determined she'd do what she could to let the children know that a house was coming soon. She didn't want them to worry. Barbara didn't want just to give them a promise, either. They'd both heard too many promises in their lives from their father, and none of them had come true. No, she wanted to show the children that she was serious.

Barbara walked over to the oven and pulled a coffee cake out of the oven. That was the last of the baked goods. Everything needed to cool for a minute and then she'd be ready to go. In the meantime, she'd go see how the weather looked outside.

Barbara didn't even bother to lie to herself as she stood in the open doorway to the outside. She was looking down the road to see if Carl was driving by anytime soon. There were several pickups parked in front of the hardware store, but there was nothing else coming down the road into town. The sheriff must have driven by earlier.

Oh, well, Barbara told herself, she had better things to do today than keep an eye out for the sheriff.

She needed to change clothes before Mrs. Hargrove picked her up in fifteen minutes, and Barbara didn't know whether to dress poor or rich. If she dressed poor, she might get more from a pawnbroker for the rings she was willing to sell. But if she dressed too poor, the pawnbroker might think the rings were stolen.

In the end, Barbara settled for wearing jeans and a sweater. She looked just like what she was, a young divorced woman who was trying to do something better for her children.

The sheriff had to go out to the Elkton ranch the first thing this morning to take a report on a fight in the bunkhouse. The two ranch hands had both been tight-lipped about the fight and the sheriff didn't see much reason to do a report when he could see the two men would be at each other when he left anyway. But the foreman insisted.

"See that you keep it to fists," the sheriff told the two men after he'd written down the notes for his report. "Remember, any knives or broken bottles—anything like that and it becomes assault with a deadly weapon."

Both men gave him a curt nod and the sheriff told himself he'd done all he could.

"I hope this isn't over a woman," the sheriff gave a guess before he walked to the bunkhouse door.

"How'd you—?" one of the ranch hands said in surprise.

The sheriff shrugged. "It's usually either money or women. I figure you both get paid about the same, so it had to be a woman."

The sheriff turned and walked back to the men. "The pity of it is that she's going to pick the loser in the fight instead of the winner anyway."

The men looked up at him in astonishment.

"Well, think about it," the sheriff said. "How do you figure it's going to go?"

The men stopped being so closemouthed soon enough as they thought about just who would end up with the woman if they kept fighting. The sheriff felt he'd done his job and he left.

All of the way back into Dry Creek, the

sheriff wished he knew an easy answer to the questions about the woman who was troubling him. He wasn't worried any more that she might be breaking the law by hiding some of her ex-husband's stolen money. But he was worried that he'd be setting himself up for a deep disappointment if he kept on dreaming the way he was.

It was almost eleven o'clock before the sheriff drove into Dry Creek for the second time that morning. He'd swung by earlier around seven o'clock and checked that Mrs. Hargrove's kitchen light was on. Then he'd gotten the call to go to the Elkton ranch and had ended up there. The sheriff knew that Barbara was going into Miles City with Mrs. Hargrove, so he didn't really expect her to answer the door when he knocked on the outside of the building that housed the dance studio and bakery.

The sheriff didn't get an answer to his knock, but he decided to walk around the building anyway. The fact that someone had left that money for the cake on the porch here without anyone hearing or seeing anything made him realize how vulnerable Barbara and the children were. It wouldn't hurt to be sure all of the windows closed securely and the door at the back was sturdy.

Once he finished looking around this building, he might even step over to the old Gossett place and have a good look at that house. Mr. Gossett had asked him to keep an eye on the place for him, and it had been a couple of months since the sheriff had made an inspection of the house to be sure everything was still locked up tight. Unless he was wrong, he thought the Gossett house would be a much sturdier building. It needed some paint, but that didn't weaken the house any.

The sheriff had finished his inspection of the building Barbara was living in and found it was in the same condition it had been in the last time he looked. It would do for the time being, but not for long.

The sheriff looked down the street a little at the Gossett house.

Mrs. Hargrove had told the sheriff that Barbara was interested in renting that house, but he hadn't given it much thought until lately. He was sure old man Gossett would want to rent the house. Why would he pass up some good income?

The sheriff left his car parked where it was and walked down the street to the Gossett house. When he came to the wooden fence surrounding the house, he reached for the lock on the inside of the gate. That was odd, he thought, as he saw that the lock was undone. The sheriff frowned; he didn't like the thought of someone nosing around the old Gossett place. It was probably just kids, but still—

The sheriff walked around the house carefully and checked that none of the windows were unlocked. No one had tampered with the two doors either. The sheriff decided he had been right and that it had been curious kids who had unlocked the gate when he noticed the papers behind one of the pine trees.

These weren't left by kids, the sheriff told himself, as he picked up the wrappers for several rolls of antacid tablets.

The sheriff thought a moment and decided that whoever had been standing here hadn't been interested in vandalism because nothing had been disturbed. There was something about an unpainted place that just attracted trouble, he finally decided. It wouldn't hurt for him to put a coat of white paint on that fence. Maybe that would stop anyone from making themselves at home in the backyard.

Barbara stood at the counter of the pawnshop and opened up the envelope that held the three rings she was selling. She was surprised that she didn't have some feelings of sadness as she rolled the rings out onto the counter of the pawn shop so that the man could look at them more closely.

Maybe she wasn't more upset about giving up the rings because she had had such a hard time finding a pawnshop. When she'd told Mrs. Hargrove that she wanted to go to a pawnshop when they got to Miles City, the older woman had said she didn't think Miles City had any pawnshops. Then Mrs. Hargrove had offered Barbara the use of her car so she could drive to Billings.

Barbara was reluctant to drive Mrs. Hargrove's car, but the older woman had finally convinced her to borrow it.

"There's some kind of a pawnshop just this side of Billings," the older woman had said.

"You can be there and back before I'm through with my appointment. It's a long one today."

Barbara hadn't told Mrs. Hargrove that she was selling the rings. She wasn't altogether sure that the older woman would approve. There seemed to be something cold about selling wedding rings. Maybe it just reminded Barbara of all that she had lost, she thought. It wasn't just the years that she had used up being married to Neal; it was also the reluctance she felt now to trust any man with her well-being or, even more important, the well-being of her children.

She might date again, Barbara admitted. But it would have to be a casual friendly thing with no expectations by her or anyone else that it would deepen into a real romantic relationship.

And, she thought, smiling to herself a little as the man in front of her kept looking at the rings, the only reason she was even willing to date a little was because she was hoping Carl would want to have dinner with her every so often. That would be nice.

"I'll give you five hundred dollars for all of them," the man behind the counter finally announced. "And I've got to be a fool to go that high. If you were a man, I'd give you four."

"I don't think that the fact that I'm—" Barbara started and then shut her mouth. Instead, she smiled. "Thank you. That sounds fair."

Barbara was grateful to get that much for the rings. She would have to pick up a newspaper and look at the classified ads. Someone surely had a sturdy dining table for sale. Maybe she would even have enough to buy some dishes and silverware as well. And a small rug for the bathroom.

Oh, Barbara thought as she took the stack of twenty-dollar bills that the man handed to her, there were so many things that she and the children could use. If she had time today, she'd try to buy a few of them.

Floyd Spencer didn't feel too good. He was sitting at his desk at the bank, but he wished with all his heart that he was home in his bed.

"How are you doing there, Floyd?"

Floyd looked up to see his manager standing beside his desk. "I'll get those reports soon."

Fortunately, he'd kept no records of the times he had tried to transfer that money to the offshore accounts for Harlow and Neal, so he had nothing on his desk he needed to hide.

His manager was frowning at Floyd anyway. "How are you feeling these days?"

"Ah, fine," Floyd mumbled. He hadn't slept for six days straight, but he didn't want to look like he was falling down on his job. He needed this job.

The manager nodded. "The Human Resources division at corporate is worried that the staff here has been suffering from stress related to that bank robbery. Even though it didn't happen here, it was close."

Floyd was worried that he might stop breathing. Was this a clue that someone suspected something? "I'm not stressed."

"It's nothing to be ashamed of." His manager sat on a corner of Floyd's desk. "I've noticed you seem a little more tired than usual. Have you been sleeping okay?"

"Ahhh." Floyd sat there like a deer in the headlights. He didn't know which way to turn.

"If you need to take a couple of days off to get some rest, don't be shy about asking. Just fill out the form," the manager finally suggested as he stood up. "You haven't taken much sick time this year."

Floyd waited for his manager to leave before he started to breathe again. He sure could use a couple of days off. Maybe he could even get his stomach to settle down.

Chapter Fifteen

When Barbara arrived at the dentist's office to meet Mrs. Hargrove, the older woman's jaw was still frozen, and she nodded in relief when Barbara offered to continue driving the car through to Dry Creek.

"'Hank 'ou,'" Mrs. Hargrove mumbled.

Barbara stopped at the grocery store before leaving Miles City and bought a bag of frozen peas so that Mrs. Hargrove could hold their coldness to her cheek.

"I always got frozen peas for the kids when they had dental work done," Barbara said as she came back from the store, carrying a bag with the vegetables and a few other items. She handed the peas to the older woman through the open window in the car.

"'Onderful," Mrs. Hargrove said as she gratefully took the peas.

At least Mrs. Hargrove let her help some, Barbara reflected as she walked around to the driver's side of the car, stopping to put the rest of the grocery bags in the backseat. Barbara was glad she could do some small service for Mrs. Hargrove. Maybe a person needed to work up to coffee-pouring around here, she reflected. Maybe it would start with a bag of frozen peas.

When Barbara slid into the driver's seat, Mrs. Hargrove reached for her purse and pulled out a five-dollar bill. "'Et me 'ay 'ou."

"You don't need to pay me for a bag of peas," Barbara said. "Neighbors borrow things like that. It's like a cup of sugar."

Mrs. Hargrove shook her head and offered the bill to Barbara again. "'Or the children."

Barbara shook her head, too. "The children and I are fine." Barbara reached into her jacket pocket and pulled out the stack of twenties. "See? We're fine."

"Ah," Mrs. Hargrove said as she lowered her five-dollar bill into her lap.

Mrs. Hargrove slept on the way back to Dry Creek, with the bag of peas pressed between the side window and her cheek. The ride was peaceful for Barbara. One thing she never got used to was all the space that there was here in southern Montana. She liked looking at these empty vistas filled with browns and grays and the blue of the sky. There wasn't much traffic on Interstate 94, so she watched the gray cloud formations in the sky as she drove. It was restful.

It was three o'clock before Barbara drove the car into Mrs. Hargrove's driveway. The sky had grown increasingly full of gray clouds as the hours passed. It felt like it should rain, but no drops had fallen.

Barbara was glad she'd sent the children to school with jackets today. It was still another hour before they'd get here on the school bus, and it might be raining by then.

One would think, she told herself, with all the rain they had had lately that some grass would be starting to grow beside the road and in the spaces between the houses around here. The ground still looked like gray and brown mud though. There weren't any leaves on the few oak trees around, either. Only the sturdy pine trees held their green needles.

Barbara helped Mrs. Hargrove into her house. Ordinarily the older woman wouldn't need any help getting anywhere, but today she seemed a little wobbly after her dental appointment.

The house was cold and Mrs. Hargrove asked Barbara to turn on the heat, so she did. The thermostat was located in the dining room.

Mrs. Hargrove's house wasn't anything special. It had a big lived-in kitchen on the first floor, along with a small living room and dining area. Upstairs, Barbara guessed, there were two large or three small bedrooms and a bathroom. Many of the walls had floral wallpaper on them, and the paper didn't always match the curtains at the windows or the rugs on the floor, but together everything looked cozy.

Barbara dreamed of having a house like this. She'd never demanded a fancy place with designer furniture. What she wanted instead was a house that had more artwork on the refrigerator than on the walls. A place where everyone felt at home and guests didn't have to take off their shoes to walk on the kitchen linoleum. A place like that would be a happy place for her children.

Maybe, she decided, she should walk past the building where she lived and go down a few houses to take another look at the old Gossett house. She needed to do something to make her dream seem as if it could happen.

The sheriff hoped the rain would hold off enough for him to finish painting at least the front of this fence. He'd bought a gallon of white outdoor paint and a couple of brushes from the hardware store an hour or so ago. He always had some old clothes in the trunk of his car for the days when he needed to do a quick chore for Mrs. Hargrove. Once he'd slipped an old sweatshirt over his uniform, he'd started painting up and down along the spikes of the old picket fence.

Surprisingly, the wood seemed to be in good shape, except for the places where a nail had come loose and the board was swinging. The sheriff would fix those later.

Maybe with a coat of paint and some nails, it would stand up for another year or so until old man Gossett's nephew decided what to do with the house.

For the time being, the sheriff hoped Barbara would be able to rent the place. It wasn't the house he figured she wanted eventually, but it would be good for the children to have something now. They needed a place to run and scream and be kids.

The sheriff had never thought much about houses until the last few days. Mostly, a house to him was just some place to sleep and keep his things. The trailer had suited him fine. Oh, a year or two ago, he had bought plans for a three-bedroom log cabin from some ad he'd seen in a magazine. He'd thought about building that log house and tucking it next to those trees on his place so the huge porch it showed in the picture would have lots of shade in the summer.

He had enough in his savings account for a down payment on the kit they sold to build the house. It included all of the materials; all he'd have to supply was the work. He already had a well and septic system on the property.

Electricity, too. It wouldn't take much to actually make that log house a reality.

But something held him back. Maybe it was just that since it was only him, he'd rather rattle around in a tin box instead of setting himself up in a house that was meant to be shared. A man could get awfully lonesome sitting on that big porch all by himself.

The sheriff wondered if that was why old man Gossett hadn't kept up his house. Maybe it had become depressing to the man when he was living all alone in it. Some things were just meant to be shared and a house was one of them. The sheriff thought about the old man as he kept painting the fence boards. Too bad Mr. Gossett hadn't started going to church, the sheriff finally decided. That would have made him feel better.

The sheriff had to admit there was something that drew a person to the church two doors down from where he stood. For the life of him, he didn't know what it was. He knew that Matthew gave some good advice in his sermons. Even if he hadn't gone there yesterday to hear one for himself, the sheriff had talked with Matthew enough over the years to know that the man had a good head on his shoulders. But just good advice didn't seem like it covered the reason why so many people seemed so content to be there.

The sheriff put his brush down on the rim of the paint can as he stood to stretch his back. He might just have to go back to that church next Sunday. Not that he wanted to help Mrs. Hargrove with her class again. Those little ones would cause him grief soon enough when they were teenagers. He wondered what the town would think if he deputized Mrs. Hargrove to keep them in line when the time came. She'd do it, too, he thought with a smile.

The sheriff heard the sounds of footsteps coming down the gravel road and turned to see Barbara walking toward him.

"Well, look who's here. I was just thinking about you," the sheriff said.

The afternoon was developing quite a chill and Barbara's cheeks were rosy from the cold. She hugged her jacket to her, her arms crossed in the wool sleeves.

She was pretty as a picture, the sheriff thought as he took a moment to enjoy the sight of her.

"Hello, Carl," Barbara said. "Are you the one who has been doing all this painting?"

Barbara had smelled the paint when she passed the hardware store. It was the smell that had made her look up to see that someone had been painting the fence around the old Gossett house.

"Want to help paint?" the sheriff asked. "I've got an extra brush and an old sweatshirt in the trunk of my car."

Barbara took a deep breath. "I've thought about painting this fence myself—just in case Mr. Gossett ever decides he can rent the house to me."

"I've been thinking the house would suit you," the sheriff said. "The inside would need some painting, too, but the rooms are sound and the ceiling is tight. No leaks that I've seen."

"You've seen inside?" Barbara asked. "I've been tempted to look in the windows, but the gate was locked and—"

The sheriff frowned. "I think someone broke the lock on the gate to get back in the trees."

"I hope it's not someone else like me who wants to rent the place," Barbara said. "I know I've been tempted to tamper with the gate."

"I don't know of anyone else who's thinking of renting it," the sheriff said.

"But as long as the gate is open," Barbara said, "I don't suppose it would be trespassing just to take a little look in the window?"

The sheriff grinned. "I'm supposed to be checking out the place now and again, so I think we can look through a few windows."

Barbara couldn't help herself. When the sheriff used a handkerchief to wipe away a spot on the window so she could see inside the kitchen of the Gossett house, she knew right where she wanted to put the table.

The kitchen was a square room, with an old refrigerator and stove pushed to one wall. The window she was looking in was over the sink. A light blue linoleum covered the floor and what looked like yellow paint covered the walls. There were no curtains on the window and only a bare bulb hanging down in the center of the room

"I want a round table for the middle right there." Barbara pointed to the place directly under the light bulb. "Maybe one of those old oak ones—you know, the ones that have leaves that you put in when you have company? I bought the classified ads so I can look and see if anyone has one to sell. It'd be perfect for Sunday dinners."

"Tables like that are hard to find," the sheriff said. "Even used they're a pretty penny."

Barbara nodded. "They're worth it though. There's a place to put a Tiffany-style lamp right over it. I can just see Bobby sitting there and doing his math homework. I should check the classifieds for a Tiffany-style lamp, too, although that's not likely to be listed."

"No, no, it's not," the sheriff said.

Barbara finally pulled herself away from the window. "Can we look in the living-room window too? I want to know what kind of a sofa to look for—it'll have to be used, of course, but there's still a pretty good selection."

The sheriff used his handkerchief to clean a circle on the next window too.

"Oh, there's still a rocking chair in there," Barbara said.

The living room was also square-shaped, but it had a nice wood floor that Barbara thought would clean up nicely. With a little wax, it would even shine. The walls in this room were such a dirty mauve that she knew it had been a long time since anyone had painted or even cleaned the walls.

"There's two fair-sized bedrooms in the back and a third one that's pretty small off the dining room," the sheriff said. "One of them has a bed in it. That was the room old man Gossett slept in. I don't think there's much in the other rooms. Maybe some old dressers."

"I can get furniture," Barbara said. She was filled with confidence. She had the money from the pawnshop in her pocket and she'd make every penny count. If she was buying used, she should be able to furnish the whole house with the money she had.

Barbara would have kept looking in the windows even longer, except she wanted to help finish painting the fence before the children came home from school. She was full of excitement herself, but she didn't want to get the children's hopes up. She didn't know, after all, if the Gossett house would ever be available for her to rent.

After they walked back to where the sheriff had left the paint and brushes, he went to his car and opened the trunk. He held up two old sweatshirts. "The black one or the purple one?"

"Purple," Barbara said as she walked over to take the sweatshirt. "It's too nice a day to wear black."

"It's going to rain."

Barbara smiled as she took off her jacket. "All the more reason to wear purple. Now, can I leave this in your trunk?"

Barbara held out her jacket to the sheriff. He took it.

"You don't want to lose anything," the sheriff said as he carefully laid her jacket in the trunk. "Jackets like this should have zip pockets."

The sheriff put his hand right over the wad of twenty-dollar bills Barbara had in her pocket, but she wasn't sure if he saw them peeking out of the fold. He must not have, she decided, because he didn't say anything.

Not that there was any reason he shouldn't see the money, she told herself. She just didn't want people to know she had sold her wedding rings. There was something so sad about it, even though, she had to admit, she'd felt pretty good since she'd sold them. Thinking of all the furniture she could buy when she moved into a house with the children made her feel as though everything was possible.

Chapter Sixteen

Floyd stopped once he arrived in Miles City, and went to the grocery store to buy graham crackers. He had seen the boy eating graham crackers one day. Floyd hoped the boy would be reasonable and understand Floyd's need to keep him for a while.

He wouldn't hurt the boy any, Floyd told himself. Some boys would even like a little holiday away from school and their mothers. The room Floyd stayed at in the motel had a video player; maybe he should rent some cartoons for the boy or something.

It wouldn't be so bad. Especially if Floyd didn't need to take the girl, too.

Of course, it'd be easier if he took both

children. He'd gotten a second note taped to his bathroom mirror last night. Again, all of Floyd's windows were secure and the new lock he had on his door had not been forced open. Whoever Harlow had working for him, the man was a professional.

Floyd didn't mind admitting he was scared.

But it would all be okay soon. Just as soon as the ex-wife got word to Neal that someone had his children, Neal would find a way to talk to Harlow. Neither of the men were in solitary confinement. They must talk. Harlow would listen to Neal, Floyd felt certain of that.

It would all work out just fine.

The sheriff wanted the night to turn to its blackest before he got up from the chair in his trailer. He'd been sitting here ever since he'd come home, trying to keep his suspicions from running around in his head. He'd seen that wad of twenties Barbara had in the pocket of her jacket.

Maybe Barbara had gotten the money someplace legitimately, but the sheriff knew she hadn't had that kind of money a couple of days ago. She'd had to walk over to the café to get change for the hundred-dollar bills that were under that geranium planter.

It looked as if Barbara had five or six hundred dollars in her pocket now. The bills had been crisp new bills, too—just the kind of bills a bank usually had.

Barbara didn't have a bank account, and she usually took her salary in cash. Since Lizette wasn't back from her honeymoon, no one had been around to pay Barbara.

The sheriff hated being suspicious, but he was. He'd almost forgotten that the FBI had asked him to watch Barbara Strong for this very reason. Those bills reminded him of his duty.

The sheriff put a jacket over his uniform before he walked to the door of his trailer and stepped outside. He didn't have a light on the outside of his trailer, so he always had to stand a bit when he first opened the door so his eyes could adjust to the dark. He shivered a little. The night air was cold and even damper than it had been earlier today. It still hadn't rained, but the air was heavy with it.

The sheriff looked over at the trees on his left. He could see the black shapes of their

branches silhouetted against the night sky.
Yesterday, when he'd come back to the
trailer, he'd gone over there and stood on
the spot where he'd thought about building
that log house. Ever since then, his eyes had
been drawn to that spot when he stepped out
of his trailer. He shook his head. He
supposed there was just no stopping a fool
from dreaming.

The sheriff could not remember a time
when he'd disliked his job—until now. Even
so, that wouldn't stop him from doing it.

The first thing he needed to do was check
under that planter on Barbara's porch. He'd
been thinking that maybe she'd just borrowed
those hundred dollar bills and taken them
somewhere to get them changed into
twenties. He couldn't fault her for that; in
fact, he was hoping that was what had
happened. If those bills were gone, he could
just go home and go to sleep.

It wasn't more than twenty minutes later
that the sheriff stood in the dark on the gravel
road that ran through Dry Creek. There were
no lights showing from any of the houses.
He'd parked his car along the side of the road

a little before he got to the buildings. Now, he would walk the rest of the way into town.

The town of Dry Creek wasn't much more than a dozen or so buildings, half on one side of the gravel road and half on the other. Not one of the buildings was anything to brag about. None of the houses had swimming pools in their backyards, in fact, they barely had backyards. Spring had not fully come to Dry Creek and there were no green lawns sprouting anywhere.

The sheriff knew Dry Creek wouldn't make it onto most maps. But it was his town and his responsibility. He had sworn to keep it safe.

The sheriff stepped off the gravel road when he came close to the building where Barbara lived. She and the children were in the back room and should be asleep by now, but he didn't want to make any unnecessary noise. The hardware store was across the street, but no one was there. The sheriff had never noticed how black the night could be in Dry Creek.

Barbara was right about them needing a streetlight, the sheriff thought as he finished walking to the steps. The planter was close to the edge of the small porch. He lifted it easily while standing on the dirt beside the porch. The night dew had already made the wood planter cold and damp.

The sheriff had good eyes. He couldn't miss the bills lying there on the porch. He saw the two hundred-dollar bills on the bottom and a couple of twenties on top. He put the planter back down.

There was nothing he could do tonight, the sheriff told himself as he started to walk back to his car. He wasn't going to wake those two kids up just so he could question their mother about laundering stolen money. Not that he'd get any sleep tonight himself.

The sheriff had to walk past the church to get to his car and he had a sudden urge to sit for a while on the steps of the church. He lowered himself until he was doing just that. Then he put his head in his hands. He figured it was as close to praying as he knew how to get. He hoped that God knew what he was so stirred up about, even if he couldn't seem to put it into words himself. The sheriff sat there for a good half hour before standing up and walking to his car. It was going to be a long night, he thought, as he slid into the driver's side of his car and turned on the heater.

Barbara woke up early. It was five o'clock in the morning and she couldn't lie in bed any longer, so she hugged her robe around her and pulled one of the folding chairs up to the folding table. She didn't want to turn a light on and wake up the children, so she reached for the classified ads section of the newspaper she had bought yesterday.

There wasn't enough light filtering in through the curtains for her to actually read the classifieds, but Barbara liked holding the pages anyway. She was as excited as the children were at Christmas, maybe more so. After she got the bakery orders out, Barbara planned to sit down with the telephone and make a few calls on items in those ads.

The children wouldn't get back from school until four o'clock this afternoon. A person could set their watch by the school bus and Barbara knew she'd be able to make a lot of calls before then. If everything went her way, she might even be able to arrange for delivery of some of the things she was buying.

Barbara smiled just thinking of the squeals the children would make when they saw real furniture in this place.

Barbara went to the stove and turned on a burner under the teakettle. She'd boil some water for tea and instant oatmeal for breakfast. Maybe she'd even make some French toast as well. It was, after all, a special morning. Who knew what delights the day could bring?

Unfortunately, after breakfast it took an extra long time for the children to get dressed because Bobby had lost a button on the shirt he wanted to wear. Barbara knew she had a needle and thread in a small tin box, but it took her a while to find the box. When they had a real house, she told herself, she'd have everything in its appointed place so she'd always know where to find anything at any time. That alone would be a luxury.

In the meantime, she was fortunate to have found the sewing tin in the suitcase with the winter coats. She'd packed up those coats a week ago when spring seemed so close. The weather now was overcast, though, and

Barbara wondered if she shouldn't bring the heavy coats back out for another week or two.

She pulled Bobby's coat out of the suitcase. "Maybe you should take this coat today."

She gave Amanda her coat as well. "It's a cold day today."

Twenty minutes later, Barbara stood on the porch and watched the children climb into the school bus. The bus held about thirty passengers, and all of the children from Dry Creek rode it to go to school in Miles City. At first, Barbara had been doubtful about leaving her children with the bus driver, but she soon saw that Bobby and Amanda made friends with the other children on the bus. Sometimes, she thought riding the bus was the best part of the day for them.

Barbara watched the school bus as it drove down the road out of Dry Creek and then she turned to go back into the building that was as much dance studio as it was bakery. Lizette had opened the dance studio before she had the bakery, so Barbara always thought of the space as a studio first and foremost.

The counter in the back room helped with the bakery operations and Barbara had three final pies in the oven. Linda said the café could use two pies regularly now that business was growing. Barbara had made an apple and a blueberry.

She smiled a little bit to herself, wondering if the sheriff would have a piece of the blueberry pie when it was at the café later. The man sure did enjoy his food.

The telephone call came just as Barbara picked up her classified ads again. She'd sat down at the folding table not two minutes earlier. It was almost eight o'clock, and the work of the day was already done.

"Hello," Barbara said as she pulled the telephone over to the table.

Barbara heard the man's breathing before he began to speak. She knew then that it was the same man who had called about the cake. She was going to hang up when the man spoke.

"I have your kids." The man's voice was low and thick, as if he was trying to disguise it.

"Amanda and Bobby!"

"Called them over, right off the bus stop. Said I had word from their father."

"That's impossible," Barbara said. Whoever that man was, he was a sick, sick individual.

"Listen," the man said.

"Mommy?"

Barbara would know Bobby's voice anywhere. "Where are you?"

"He doesn't know," the man said with a chuckle. "But don't worry about it. You'll have them both back soon enough if you do what I say."

"I'll do anything," Barbara whispered. She knew that wasn't a good negotiating tactic, but she wanted the man to know she would do whatever he asked. "I have a few hundred dollars—"

The man laughed louder. "That's nothing."

"I could borrow—"

"Lady, I'm not asking for money. All I want is for you to go to your ex-husband and tell him he's got to get Harlow to give me more time. Tell him to stop whoever is leaving those notes for me. But first call the school and tell them your kids are out sick."

The man was crazy, Barbara thought, but at least he asked for something she could do. "I can take that message to Neal."

"Oh, and don't tell anyone. You understand me? No cops. And call the school."

Barbara nodded. "Yes, of course."

"Just tell Neal I've got his kids."

The man hung up before Barbara could say anything else.

Barbara sat at the table, frozen with the telephone in her hand. Please, don't let her children's fate rest with Neal, she thought to herself. She had no idea if Neal would care enough to do anything for the children.

Maybe the man would call back later and she could tell him to ask for something else. No, she realized, she couldn't wait for the man to call. She would have to get a message to Neal.

Barbara was already dressed in blue jeans and a cotton blouse, so she just pulled her own winter jacket out of the suitcase and put it on. At least she'd given the kids their winter jackets this morning. She'd hate to think they were cold wherever they were.

There was only one way for her to get a message to Neal, Barbara knew. She had to go to the prison in Billings and ask to see him the way she'd done on Saturday. She could only hope that Mrs. Hargrove would let her borrow the car again today.

Barbara was almost to the door when she

remembered the money in her other jacket. She went back and pulled it out of the pocket. She might need it.

The sheriff had gotten a phone call from an old rancher north of Dry Creek around seven o'clock in the morning. The man wasn't technically in the sheriff's territory, but he wanted help and the sheriff never turned anyone away. The man thought someone might be stealing cattle from him, and he wanted the sheriff to come and look around.

Since he hadn't been able to sleep, the sheriff was happy to have an excuse to drive up into that country. Some of the winter frost still clung to the ground there. Later, green would start spreading along the hills, but until then the dead grass of last year lay flattened to the ground, giving the hills their dried brown look.

It didn't take the sheriff long to find a break in the fence, and the man found his cattle not too far from there. By then, the sheriff realized that the man was just lonely so he accepted the rancher's offer to have a cup of coffee with him after they'd chased the cattle back into his pasture.

It was a gloomy day, and the sheriff didn't mind sharing part of it with another lonesome soul.

When he'd procrastinated as much as he could, the sheriff headed into Dry Creek. He had to question Barbara Strong, and he'd just as soon do it while the children were in school. The thought of what he had to do made the air feel cold, and the sheriff put his heater on for the drive into town.

The sheriff pulled into town at the same time that Barbara was walking down the street toward Mrs. Hargrove's house. Actually, the sheriff noticed, it would be more accurate to say Barbara was running.

Although the sheriff didn't want the children around when he talked to Barbara, he didn't mind talking to the woman in front of Mrs. Hargrove. The older woman could pick a liar out better than anyone he'd seen, including himself. She probably got it from all of her years teaching Sunday school. Not that it mattered much where Mrs. Hargrove got her skill. The sheriff could use another set of eyes. He didn't trust himself on this one.

Chapter Seventeen

Barbara was breathing hard when she knocked on the front door of Mrs. Hargrove's house. She usually went to the older woman's back door, but today Barbara didn't want to take the extra time to walk around the house when the front door was right there. The middle section of the door had a glass panel with a lace curtain hanging over it.

Barbara knew her face was red from walking in the cold, and she hoped that would explain the tears that kept slipping from her eyes. She needed to appear normal enough to ask Mrs. Hargrove about borrowing her car without raising the older woman's suspicions that anything was wrong. If Mrs. Hargrove thought something was wrong, she wouldn't let up until she knew what it was. Barbara knew she couldn't tell anyone.

The man on the phone hadn't specifically said she couldn't tell Mrs. Hargrove about the danger to her children, but Barbara didn't want to take any chances. *Oh, Bobby and Amanda,* she thought, *hang on.*

Barbara heard the sounds of Mrs. Hargrove walking across her wooden floor toward the door at the same time that she heard a car pull in front of Mrs. Hargrove's house. Barbara didn't even turn around to see who had come to visit Mrs. Hargrove. She just hoped that whoever it was would distract the older woman so she didn't look too carefully at Barbara's face.

"Well, hello, dear," Mrs. Hargrove said when she opened the door. "Come in out of the cold."

Mrs. Hargrove was wearing a pink gingham dress with a zipper up the front. She wore a navy cardigan sweater over the dress and a white apron around her waist. Her gray hair was wrapped around soft green curlers and her feet were in tennis shoes.

"I have hot water on the stove, dear, if you'd like a cup of tea," the older woman said as she stepped back into the house so Barbara could enter.

Barbara knew Mrs. Hargrove had seen the distress on her face. She shook her head and stayed where she was. "I'm in a hurry, but I do have a favor to ask."

Mrs. Hargrove nodded. "What can I do?"

Barbara heard the footsteps behind her. Whoever had stopped to visit would be at the top of the steps soon. Barbara knew she needed to get her request out there quickly. Maybe then the other person could distract Mrs. Hargrove.

"I'd like to borrow your car." Barbara tried to keep the desperation out of her voice. "I need to drive into Billings."

Barbara knew someone stood on the step beside her. She didn't even need to turn her head to know it was the sheriff. She could see the brim of his hat out of the side of her eye. She felt a sudden gladness that he was there, until she realized that she couldn't tell him anything about what was wrong. That man had said he would hurt her children if she told a cop. The sheriff was the last person she could tell.

"I can take you to Billings," the sheriff offered.

He must not like her asking to use Mrs. Hargrove's car, Barbara thought. She couldn't think of any other reason for the cold edge in his voice.

"I'm planning to pay for the gas, of course," Barbara added. She'd filled the gas tank before for Mrs. Hargrove. "And give her maybe twenty or so extra for—" Barbara spread her hands "—wear on the tires and all."

"Oh, but you don't—" Mrs. Hargrove began.

"You're sure free with your money these days," the sheriff said. He drew the words out, and there wasn't a friendly sound in any of them. "Did you get a raise or something?"

"Carl!" Mrs. Hargrove sounded startled.

Barbara blushed even more at the tone in the sheriff's voice. She stepped farther away from him so she could turn and look at his face fully.

"I don't have time to stand here and talk about my salary," Barbara said. She needed to focus on the children. She used to be good at putting a mask on to hide her feelings when Neal started yelling at her. She'd never thought she'd have to use it with the sheriff.

"Of course, you don't, dear," Mrs. Hargrove said as she reached out a hand toward Barbara. "Just give me a minute to get the keys to my car."

Mrs. Hargrove stepped farther back into her house. Barbara wished the sheriff would go inside with her neighbor. Or turn around and leave. She didn't see any need for him to keep standing with her in front of Mrs. Hargrove's door. They looked like salespeople.

"I never did ask you how Neal was doing the other day," the sheriff finally said.

"You might not have, but your friends did," Barbara said wearily. She hadn't really minded all of the questions the staff at the prison had asked about Neal. She was open to telling them anything she knew.

The sheriff nodded. "I don't suppose he had a message for the children or anything. Something you forgot to tell the others."

"I didn't forget anything."

Ten minutes ago, Barbara had believed she

was building a life here. But she had been wrong. Everything was slipping away. She'd thought she and the children were safe in Dry Creek. She'd been wrong about that. She'd thought she would make friends here; she was beginning to wonder if that would ever happen.

She'd even started to think the sheriff was different from other men she'd known. It looked like she'd been wrong about that, too.

Barbara kept looking straight ahead until Mrs. Hargrove came back with the keys.

"Here it is dear." The older woman held out the key ring to Barbara.

"Is there anything you'd like to tell me before you go?" the sheriff asked stiffly.

Barbara shook her head as she took the keys from Mrs. Hargrove.

"Is there trouble?" Mrs. Hargrove asked as her eyes went back and forth from the sheriff to Barbara.

"Everything's fine," Barbara said. "I just need to go into Billings."

"I'm asking again if I can drive you," the sheriff said.

Barbara shook her head. She kept her hand curled around those keys. She didn't know what she would do if Mrs. Hargrove asked for them back.

"You're not sick, are you, dear?" Mrs. Hargrove asked anxiously. "If you've got some bad news from a doctor or something, you shouldn't be by yourself. I could go with you."

"I'm fine alone," Barbara said. She did smile at the older woman, however. At least Mrs. Hargrove was being kind, unlike the other person standing here. "I haven't heard from any doctor. My health is good."

Unless you counted the fact that her heart was being squeezed by fear, Barbara thought to herself.

"But you don't need to be alone," Mrs. Hargrove insisted as she reached behind the door. "I've got my purse right here. I think it's best if I come with you."

"Oh, no, I couldn't—that is, I'll be fine without—" Barbara stammered.

Mrs. Hargrove was already stepping out onto her porch and pulling her door shut behind her. "It's no problem. I could use some more peppermints anyway. I like to keep them on hand for guests."

"I thought you had water boiling for tea,"

Barbara said. There had to be some sane reason why Mrs. Hargrove couldn't go.

"I turned it off when I got the keys," Mrs. Hargrove said as she walked between Barbara and the sheriff to head down her steps. "I like to be ready for what the day holds. Sometimes God just gives me a feeling that tells me to go, and that's when I head out. Like now."

Mrs. Hargrove turned around to grin at Barbara and the sheriff. Barbara felt something shift in the sheriff's manner, and she looked him in the face again. He gave her a wry smile.

At least, Barbara thought, the sheriff was looking her in the eye again.

"I thought that was just your arthritis talking," the sheriff said as he turned to Mrs. Hargrove. "It does look like rain out."

"Don't you be doubting the Lord's leading, Carl Wall. You'll see for yourself what I'm talking about someday." Mrs. Hargrove clucked as she made her way down her steps and then looked back up the stairs. "Well, is anyone else coming or not?"

Barbara figured there had to be some way

to be in the same car with Mrs. Hargrove for the long drive into Billings without telling the older woman what was happening. She might even find it comforting just to have someone sitting beside her as she worried about Bobby and Amanda.

The sheriff decided he should just deputize Mrs. Hargrove one of these days and be done with it. He watched as the two women drove off in Mrs. Hargrove's old rattletrap of a car. The muffler was blowing a little smoke, but he was sure that wouldn't stop the women. If he ever needed backup, he should remember Mrs. Hargrove did a fine job of picking up the slack.

Barbara wasn't a mile out of Dry Creek before she saw that there was a car following her. It was the sheriff's car, of course. At first, she thought she was just being paranoid, and that he was just going in the same direction as she was. There was, after all, only one road between Dry Creek and the interstate. Barbara deliberately slowed down so the sheriff could pass. He didn't pass her. She sped up and he went faster.

"He's following us," Barbara said indignantly.

Mrs. Hargrove nodded brightly. "I thought he might. Carl's a man of strong emotions."

Barbara didn't want to argue with Mrs. Hargrove, especially not when she was sitting in the woman's car, but she couldn't let the older woman weave any fantasies either. "I don't think this is about his emotions."

Barbara didn't want to press her foot to the gas pedal too hard. She'd noticed that the muffler was making a little noise. The whole car shook some, but she supposed that was only to be expected given the car's age.

"You never did tell me how you got this car," Barbara said. That should give Mrs. Hargrove something to talk about. It was a safe topic.

"It used to belong to Mr. Gossett," the older woman said. "He gave it to me one year for Christmas. He said it was to pay me back for all the loaves of plum bread I'd given to him over the years."

The older woman smiled. "Of course, I refused, even though the car wasn't worth much back then either. It's a 1971, you know."

"What changed your mind?" Barbara looked in the rearview mirror. The sheriff was still there.

"He started trying to bake *me* loaves of plum bread," the older woman said and then chuckled. "He was determined to pay me back, and I feared he'd burn his house down if he kept trying to bake."

Even the thought of Mr. Gossett's house couldn't get Barbara's mind to relax. She felt as if someone had come along and twisted her whole body into knots. "Do you really think it's going to rain?"

Barbara didn't know if Bobby and Amanda were being kept outdoors or not. They could catch pneumonia if it rained. The nights were still so cold around here.

"Is rain what's bothering you?"

Barbara shook her head. "Just curious."

"I see," Mrs. Hargrove said as she looked straight ahead.

The older woman was silent for a while. "The windshield wipers don't work very well. I don't think I told you that. I was going to have Carl fix them when he fixes the muffler."

Barbara nodded. She had refused to look

in the rearview mirror for the past five minutes, and her neck was beginning to ache from the tension of keeping her head from doing what it wanted to do. Oh, well. She looked up to steal a glance at the mirror. The sheriff was still there.

"If the sheriff isn't coming along because of his emotions, is it because it's his duty?" Mrs. Hargrove quietly asked.

Barbara didn't move a muscle.

Mrs. Hargrove waited a minute. "Sometimes people think that if they've done something against the law there's no hope, but the law is there as much to help as to hurt. It gives a person a chance to make a new beginning."

"I can't tell you what's wrong," Barbara finally said. If she didn't admit that much, Mrs. Hargrove would be digging away at her until they got to Billings.

The older woman nodded. "Well, if it comes the time when you can tell me, I'm here to listen."

"Thank you," Barbara said.

"I know how hard it is to trust again when someone has betrayed you," Mrs. Hargrove said.

Barbara swallowed. "It's not that I don't trust—"

Barbara stopped. She couldn't even finish that sentence. Of course she didn't trust anyone. The man on the phone had told her not to tell the cops, but Barbara acknowledged to herself that she wouldn't have told anyone anyway. She was used to solving her own problems. Or trying to, at least. For the first time in a long time, she wished it weren't so. She'd give anything to have a friend who could share this burden. She was afraid to even mention Bobby's or Amanda's names for fear she'd start to cry and it would all spill out.

"Trust was one of the hardest things I had to learn, too," Mrs. Hargrove said as she opened the purse she held on her lap and rummaged around inside it. Finally, she pulled out a roll of butterscotch candy. She held the roll out to Barbara. "Want one?"

Barbara shook her head.

Mrs. Hargrove nodded and then unwrapped one of the candies and put it in her mouth. "Took me a long time to trust God. I finally realized I couldn't do it until I learned to trust people some first. So, I started with my husband." Mrs. Hargrove smiled. "But you don't want to hear an old woman's story."

"Yes, I do," Barbara said before she saw the gleam in the older woman's eyes and realized she'd fallen for the bait.

Mrs. Hargrove began to talk, and Barbara let the words flow over her. It was soothing. The older woman talked about her days as a newly married woman who'd just moved to the small town of Dry Creek. Mrs. Hargrove was an undemanding storyteller and was content with Barbara's occasional comments. It gave Barbara time to worry about Bobby and Amanda in peace. And to think about trust. The more the older woman talked, the more Barbara wanted to tell someone that a bad man had her children and it was all up to Barbara to save them.

She just felt so inadequate, Barbara admitted to herself. The reason she didn't trust others was not because she thought she didn't need anyone or that she should do it all by herself. She just did not have any faith that anyone would help.

There was a flash of red, and Barbara looked in the rearview mirror.

"What's—" Barbara started to say.

The sheriff had just turned on his siren.

Barbara pulled over. She drummed her fingers on the steering wheel as she waited for the sheriff to walk up beside the car and motion for her to roll down her window.

"I wasn't speeding," Barbara said when she rolled down the window. "You can ask Mrs. Hargrove here."

"Hi, Carl," the older woman said as she looked over to see the sheriff, who had bent down so his face could be seen in the driver's-side window.

"I know you weren't speeding," the sheriff said. "I just thought I should get that muffler hooked on a little better or you're going to be blowing black smoke here soon. Then I'd have to give you a ticket for polluting the air."

"We don't have time," Barbara said.

"It'll only take fifteen minutes," the sheriff said. "The thing needs to cool off a little before I do anything. Why don't you pull off on that road up ahead? There's a couple of trees down in that coulee. You and Mrs. Hargrove could take a little walk."

"I have a can of peaches in the trunk," Mrs. Hargrove said. "We could have a picnic."

The older woman was already reaching up and unwrapping the curlers she'd worn all morning.

"That's the spirit," the sheriff said as he stood back up. "I'll meet you there."

Barbara rolled her window back up. "The muffler's not that bad. He didn't have to stop us now."

"Oh, I agree," the older woman said as she took out her last curler. "Like I say. It's his emotions."

"Well, if you count emotions as being stubborn, nosy, and hard to understand, then I guess it is."

Mrs. Hargrove chuckled. "My husband and I went on a picnic with nothing but peaches back when we were courting." The older woman looked sideways at Barbara. "Of course, that was before I'd learned to trust him."

Barbara nodded. She hoped that man on the phone would understand about a lunch break. She supposed she should be glad that it was only going to take fifteen minutes.

Before long, the sheriff slid out from under Mrs. Hargrove's car, stood up and wiped his hands on a rag he kept in his trunk for such purposes. They didn't have a highway patrol near Dry Creek and the sheriff had found it useful to learn a fair amount about fixing cars. Sometimes there just wasn't a tow truck around that could come and the sheriff was the only official who was there to help.

Of course, he always worked on Mrs. Hargrove's car anyway. He figured it would be good experience if he ever wanted to work for a museum. The mustard-colored car had been around for over thirty years, and its outside was starting to fade to a dirty yellow. The car's inside, under the hood, didn't bear thinking about.

Anyway, fixing a car always steadied him some, and he wanted to see how Mrs. Hargrove and Barbara were coming along. He looked down the slight incline where the two women had walked. Mrs. Hargrove had found a small blanket in her trunk and Barbara was spreading it on the ground now.

The sheriff figured that, unless it was something illegal, Mrs. Hargrove would get

Barbara to talk about what was wrong. So far, that hadn't happened. He didn't have a good feeling about the situation at all. Barbara wasn't the kind of person to panic over nothing. And he could see that she was just about as rattled as a person could be without spilling any secrets. He knew he should be pressing her to talk, but he just couldn't do it.

And that was why, the sheriff told himself as he started to climb down the shallow incline to where the women were, a sheriff needed to forget about having any friends.

Chapter Eighteen

Barbara could still taste the peach juice on her lips when they got into Billings. The sheriff was still following them and Mrs. Hargrove was still being so nice that Barbara wanted to cry. It was all too much.

Barbara parked the car on a side street next to the prison. The sheriff parked his car right behind her.

"Will you stay with Mrs. Hargrove?" Barbara asked as she opened the car door and saw the sheriff already walking toward their car.

Barbara noticed that the coldness had left the sheriff's face. Now, he looked more weary and sad than anything else.

"I'm the sheriff. You can tell me what's wrong."

Barbara shook her head. "I can't be seen with you. Don't follow me inside."

The sheriff nodded. "You have your rights. I can't stop you from trying to see your ex-husband."

"*Trying* to see him?" Barbara looked up. She'd never thought about being refused admittance. "They can't stop me, can they?"

"He is in jail," the sheriff said. "They let you talk to him the other day because they were hoping he would tell you something."

"But I need to talk to him—I—"

Barbara couldn't stand there any longer. She turned her back and started walking down the street to the prison.

"I'll call and ask them to let you talk to him," the sheriff said.

Barbara turned around when the sheriff spoke. "Thank you."

The sheriff nodded.

Once Barbara was inside the prison's main office, she knew she wouldn't have been allowed to see her ex-husband if the sheriff hadn't called. It wasn't the right time of day, and Neal wasn't scheduled for visitors anyway. They told her she'd have to wait almost a half hour, but they did agree to let her see him.

Neal looked surprised to see her. "I wondered who was here."

Barbara waited for Neal to be seated at the Plexiglas division and for the guard to walk away before she began to speak. "I need to talk to you. A man called on the phone. He has Bobby and Amanda and he says you have to talk to Harlow somebody and ask Harlow for more time. And to stop sending the notes. The notes were important."

Neal's surprise deepened and then turned to caution. "Who told you I know any Harlow?"

"Please, Neal, you need to help. The children are in trouble."

"Is this some kind of a trap?" Neal looked over his shoulder at the guard.

"Please, Neal, these are your children. They could be cold or worse."

Barbara had never begged Neal for anything in their years of marriage. But she didn't care any longer. She couldn't afford her pride when her children needed her. "Please, please—I'm so afraid of what will happen."

Neal snorted. "You don't even know that some man has the kids."

"I heard Bobby's voice on the phone. Please—I—"

Neal stood up and turned to the guard. "I need to go back now."

Barbara watched as her ex-husband walked away from the partition. She'd never felt so much despair in all her days of knowing Neal. How could a father abandon his children this way?

Finally, Neal disappeared behind the prison door, and Barbara was the only one left at the Plexiglas divider. She slowly got up and started to walk to the door. For the first time, she was glad that Mrs. Hargrove had come with her into Billings. Barbara didn't know if she'd have the strength to drive the car back alone.

The prison didn't clank as much as she expected, Barbara thought to herself as she walked down the hall to the main office. But the floor was squeaky, and it did smell. She would never forget what hopelessness smelled like.

The air outside the prison was as chilly as

it had been when Barbara had entered the place almost an hour ago. She hoped the children remembered to zip up their jackets so they wouldn't be cold.

The sidewalk led Barbara down toward where she had parked Mrs. Hargrove's car. There was no grass anywhere.

When Barbara could see Mrs. Hargrove's car, she saw a man standing outside it with his back facing her. The man was leaning in the window and talking to Mrs. Hargrove. It looked like the sheriff, only Barbara knew it couldn't be. The man wasn't wearing a uniform.

As Barbara walked closer, she saw that the man was wearing a light denim shirt and darker denim jeans. A leather belt curled around his waist. One of the ranch hands from Dry Creek must be in Billings, Barbara thought.

It wasn't until she got closer and the man stood up and saw her that she recognized him.

It was the sheriff.

Barbara had hoped to be able to get into the car without having an argument with him. Maybe she still could, she thought. The sheriff must be planning to stay in Billings and socialize or something. He was certainly never without his uniform in Dry Creek.

The sheriff didn't say anything as she walked closer. He just watched her.

Finally, when she was only a few feet away he spoke. "How did it go?"

Barbara nodded. "Fine."

There was a silence. Barbara looked at the ground.

"I figure you don't want to talk to me because I'm the sheriff."

Barbara looked up when he said that.

"But I was wondering if you could talk to me if I was your friend, Carl."

Barbara blinked back a tear only to have another one fight to fall.

"I know you're in trouble, and I'd like to help. As your friend."

Barbara hiccupped.

"I even went to a store and bought new clothes so I wouldn't scare you with the uniform."

Barbara nodded. "They're nice."

Finally, Carl opened his arms wide.

Barbara couldn't help herself. She threw

herself into his arms. "Someone has my children and I don't know what to do."

The tears were all over her face by now, Barbara noticed as she tried to wipe them away. She no longer felt chilled once Carl wrapped his arms around her. When she talked, she talked into his shoulder.

Carl rocked her a little as he stood there. "We'll find them. I promise."

"You can't promise," Barbara said as she attempted to raise her head from his shoulder. "No one can promise."

"I can," he whispered. "I'll find them."

Barbara was too exhausted to make any decisions. But that was okay, because Carl was doing everything that was needed. He called another sheriff he knew and arranged for the man to drive the county car back to Dry Creek. At the same time, he told the man that there had been a kidnapping, but that he didn't want a lot of uniformed officers walking around Dry Creek as that could endanger the children who were missing. They made arrangements for one officer, who was already near Dry Creek on some other business, to go there now, and others would come later.

Then Carl insisted on driving Mrs. Hargrove's car back home.

"Barbara can't be seen in my car," he told the older woman, and she nodded as though that explained everything.

"If your legs would fit in the backseat, I'd offer to drive so the two of you could sit together back there," Mrs. Hargrove said.

"I don't mind a muscle cramp or two," Carl said. "But I thought Barbara would need to rest."

Mrs. Hargrove shrugged. "Seems to me she could rest just fine on one of those big shoulders of yours."

Barbara wondered when they would stop talking about her as if she weren't there. She didn't protest too much though, especially not when Carl settled her in the backseat with his arm around her and her head on his shoulder.

"Now, tell me everything you can think of that might help the kids," Carl said as Mrs. Hargrove started the car.

Barbara told Carl everything she could think of, from the eerie feeling she'd had that they were being watched to the color of the socks that Bobby and Amanda had each worn to school today.

"Did you think to call the pastor while you were making your calls?" Mrs. Hargrove asked as she stopped at a traffic light. "Tell him we have a request for the prayer chain and that some little children need help urgently. The pastor will understand when you say we can't name names. But he'll get the calls going."

"What's a prayer chain?" Barbara asked.

"It's a telephone list we use when we have an emergency prayer request. Each person on the list calls the person below them on the list until everyone knows they need to be praying."

"They would all pray for Amanda and Bobby?"

Mrs. Hargrove snorted as the light changed and she started the car forward. "They prayed for Charley's bunions; they'll pray for Amanda and Bobby."

Barbara couldn't imagine a whole town that would care about someone's feet enough to spend two minutes thinking about them, let alone praying about them.

"Does it work?"

Mrs. Hargrove was out on the open road now. "Well, we're still waiting on the bunions. The doctor says that Charley needs to give up his boots to get rid of the bunions. So now we're praying about the boots. Giving up his boots would be a big change for Charley."

Carl made the call to the pastor. "A couple of other sheriffs—undercover—are coming to help me for a bit. The first one will be there in ten minutes. I'm going to ask him to go look in the pine trees on the old Gossett place. There's some wrappers for antacid tablets there. I'd appreciate it if you'd point out to him where the Gossett place is. Then see if anyone knows where a person can buy that brand of antacid tablets around here. Sorry I can't tell you more. But I appreciate it."

Once the call was made, there was silence in the car.

Barbara kept searching her mind for anything she could remember that would help her children. "They're just so little."

Carl nodded. "We'll find them."

Barbara raised her head from Carl's shoulder long enough to wipe at the damp place that had absorbed her tears. "Sorry about getting you all wet."

Carl's arm tightened around her. "Denim dries."

That made Barbara want to cry some more.

The town of Dry Creek came into view as the sun had almost set. Barbara realized she'd never driven into town at quite this hour. The sky was deep pink from what was left of the sunset. The whole town was lit up; it looked as though a light was turned on brightly in every room of every store and house in town.

"What's happening?" Barbara asked as they saw the lights.

Even the church was lit up. Barbara looked more closely. Maybe it was lit up even brighter than the other buildings. And cars were parked everywhere around the church. "Is there a meeting at the church?"

"Not that I know of," Mrs. Hargrove said as she drove the car past her house and stopped outside the church. "Let's see what it is."

Barbara nodded. She wondered if something else bad had happened in Dry Creek. Maybe someone was sick or something.

The three of them went into the church together. It was Mrs. Hargrove though who asked Jacob what was happening. Jacob was standing beside the door with his hat in his hands.

"There's some little kids in trouble," Jacob whispered. "Some of the women are praying. We think they might be lost somewhere. So we lit all the lights in town so they can see us if they come close, and the men and the women who are up to riding are out on horses looking for any strays."

"They're not lost," Barbara said and couldn't speak anymore. She had never known anyone to care about her and the children this much. They didn't even know it was Amanda and Bobby who were missing. They were ready to help any little children who needed them.

"They're not?" Jacob scratched his head. "We thought that when that other sheriff came asking about those wrappers for antacid pills that the children had left them in some kind of a trail. That sheriff wouldn't tell us nothing about what was going on."

Jacob looked at Carl indignantly. "You might speak to him about that."

Carl nodded. "I might. Did he find out anything about those wrappers?"

"Marlene Olson said they sold that brand at the grocery store where her cousin works in Miles City. Not every store carries them, she said. Seemed proud of the fact, like it was some big deal," Jacob said.

"Is that the Country Market?" the sheriff asked.

Jacob nodded. "That's the one all right."

Barbara felt Carl pull away from her. "I've got to go change and do a few things," he said. "I'll leave you here with Mrs. Hargrove."

"You don't need to worry about me," Barbara said.

"I know." Carl smiled. "Maybe I want to though."

Barbara didn't have an answer to that. Maybe she didn't need one, she thought, as she watched Carl walk away.

"How long did it take you to trust your husband?" Barbara asked, turning to Mrs. Hargrove.

The older woman smiled. "About as long as it will take you to trust Carl."

Barbara sat in a church pew until the night

was deep. Mrs. Hargrove and several of the other women still sat in the church, sometimes praying and sometimes singing a song. Barbara wondered how she could feel such contentment and such anxiety all at the same time.

"I've made some more tea," Mrs. Hargrove whispered as she came over and sat beside Barbara. "Are you sure you won't have some? Linda brought over some pie, too."

"Oh, the bakery stuff," Barbara suddenly remembered. "I never made any of the deliveries this morning."

"Don't worry," Mrs. Hargrove said. "You can have a day-old sale tomorrow."

"Today, you mean," Barbara said. The last time she had looked at her watch it had been one o'clock in the morning. Carl had been gone for over six hours now. "I wonder if Bobby and Amanda are sleeping."

Mrs. Hargrove put her hand on Barbara's arm and squeezed it.

The phone rang somewhere in the distance.

"That'll be in the pastor's study," Mrs. Hargrove said as she stood up. "I'll go answer it."

"It could be Carl," Barbara said as she rose, too.

The two women walked to the back room.

The phone call was from one of the men working at the Elkton ranch. He'd been trying to call his sister in Miles City. It was a wrong number.

"Tonight of all nights," Mrs. Hargrove muttered sympathetically as she put her arm around Barbara and they walked back toward the main part of the church.

The church had long windows that rose above the pews on both sides. They were frosted so no one could see through them clearly. In the front of the church there was a large cross.

Barbara felt she'd found a home here tonight in this church. Even if she didn't find all of the answers she needed, she'd found a comfort within these walls. She didn't walk reluctantly back to the main room. Mrs. Hargrove had told her they called the room the sanctuary and she thought it was a fitting name.

The pastor's study was joined to the sanctuary by a hall, and the two women had almost finished walking the length of the hallway when the door at the back of the sanctuary opened. Barbara didn't see the door open because she was still in the hallway, but she heard it.

"Mommy," she heard Bobby's voice call out softly.

"Oh," Barbara said as she ran through the doorway and into the sanctuary. At the back of the room Bobby stood with his hand in Carl's. Amanda was curled up asleep in Carl's other arm.

"Oh," Barbara said again as she raced down the aisle to meet them.

Bobby let go of Carl's hand and flung himself into Barbara's arms as she knelt down to hug him. Barbara breathed in the smell of her boy and ran her hands over his back and his arms to be sure he was okay. By then Amanda had awakened and was reaching for her mother as well.

"Thank you." Barbara looked up to Carl as she held her arms out for Amanda. "Thank you so much."

Carl nodded. "We arrested the man who had them, and I still have some paperwork to do that will require me talking to them, but, for tonight, you can take them home and put them to bed. They've had a long day."

"Thank you." Barbara repeated herself. She wished she knew something clever to say to thank Carl, but she didn't. "Thank you so much."

Barbara spent the rest of the night just watching Bobby and Amanda sleep. She had such a sense of gratitude for their well-being. It didn't seem sufficient just to thank the sheriff. She knew that part of tonight's rescue was due to the prayers and concern of the people of Dry Creek as well. She didn't even know how to thank the sheriff adequately; she had no idea whatsoever about how to thank God. For now, she'd just have to be content with the feeling she had that He knew. Tomorrow, she'd ask Mrs. Hargrove to help her say a prayer of thanks.

The next morning dawned slowly. A pink blush swept the sky before gray clouds pushed it away. Barbara had baked goods she needed to prepare for today and the children had school. Perhaps, though, she thought, they all needed a day of rest. Barbara would do the standing orders for the bakery, but she would keep the children home from school. In fact, until she found out more about how they had disappeared from school, she wasn't sure she was comfortable with sending them back anyway.

Bobby was the one who told Barbara how it all happened. The bus had gotten to school a little earlier than usual and Bobby had followed Amanda off the bus. Amanda was the one who first heard the man in the car saying he had a message for them from their father. Amanda started to walk over and Bobby followed her.

"I was like Daniel," Bobby informed Barbara proudly when she served him some scrambled eggs at breakfast. "I just trusted God that no lion would get me and Amanda."

"There's no lions around here, silly," Amanda giggled.

Barbara was glad Amanda didn't seem to realize the dangers they had faced.

Barbara had already hugged her children so many times last night and this morning that Bobby was becoming indignant about it. Instead of giving him another hug, she smiled at him. "I trusted Him, too."

Barbara wondered if trust always came from desperation.

"I trusted the sheriff too," Bobby added, his eyes shining. "And his gun. He had that gun aimed right at the man who took me."

"I'm sure the sheriff is very careful with his gun," Barbara said. "Guns are not toys."

Bobby nodded. "And he let me run the siren on the way home."

Barbara smiled. It was good to have her children back.

Chapter Nineteen

Several days later, the sheriff stood at his closet door and wondered what to wear. He was worse than some debutante at her first ball. He'd pulled his suit out and it was lying on his bed. It didn't seem the right thing to wear for what he had in mind. He'd already passed on wearing his uniform.

He had an old T-shirt from a Miles City bowling league he'd joined once. He supposed that made him look like a man who had interests, but he'd only bowled a few games before he realized he didn't really like rolling a ball down a lane.

He had a few white cotton shirts that he

wore with his suit, but they seemed a little boring when all was said and done.

That left the denim shirt and jeans. He was wishing now he'd bought the shirt with the pearl snaps instead of the ordinary buttons. He hadn't realized until he started to get dressed tonight that he had such an unexciting wardrobe. Oh, well, the denim would do, even with the buttons. It would be getting dark before long anyway.

It was Saturday night, and the sheriff was taking Barbara to dinner again. He was more nervous than he had any right to be when she'd already decided she only saw him as a friend. But, the night was clear and full of promise. It was warm enough that everyone knew spring was really here. And women sometimes changed their minds.

He'd seen Barbara every day this week, and each time she'd thanked him for what he'd done to bring her children back. The sheriff tried to tell her he'd only been doing his job. It hadn't even been difficult really. The tip on the antacid wrapper had led him to the Country Market, which had led him to the motel next door. The motel clerk had said the man in unit 314 had brought two children with him on this trip. All the sheriff had needed to do was go knock on the door.

The day after the children came home, the sheriff and Barbara had both sat with Bobby and Amanda while the sheriff asked questions for the report he needed to file. When the sheriff had mentioned his suspicions about the money she had, Barbara had willingly told him about selling her wedding rings. She'd even shown him the receipt the pawnshop had given her before telling him once again how very grateful she was.

"You don't need to keep thanking me," the sheriff had said for the third time that day. "It's my job to arrest kidnappers."

"It wasn't your job to let Amanda wear your hat on the way back," she'd said. "Or to tell Bobby what a brave boy he'd been."

"Well, they are brave kids," the sheriff protested. "I wouldn't lie to them."

"I know," Barbara said with another smile. "That's why I'm thanking you."

The sheriff had waited all week for the thank-you's to die down. He didn't want

Barbara to feel so grateful to him that she stopped being herself.

The sheriff looked at himself in the mirror. The denim shirt did look a little plain, he thought, as he reached for the brass name tag that the department had issued him. This might dress it up a bit.

Before he left the trailer, the sheriff picked up a manila envelope that was on the bookcase by his door. He also picked up the long-stemmed red rose he'd bought earlier today in Miles City. The rose had one of those little tubes on the end of it and the clerk had told him the rose would stay fresh for hours with no other water. It's amazing what nature could do, the sheriff thought as he closed and locked his door with one hand.

As always, he paused on the steps of his trailer and his eyes strayed to that spot in the trees where he planned to build. Before long, the grass would be growing there. He might even plant a rosebush over there now so it'd be mature when he got around to building the log house.

Barbara sat down at the oak table that she had bought to replace the folding one. She'd bought four chairs to go with it as well. Sometimes she sat down at the table just for the sheer pleasure of running her hands over the wood top and feeling how sturdy it was. Mrs. Hargrove had given her four placemats for the table and Barbara kept one under the vase she'd bought and kept in the center of the table.

Spring had started to warm up Dry Creek. Barbara had seen a few stalks of grass in the past few days. Before long, there would be flowers around and she'd bought the vase so she'd be ready to pick some wildflowers.

Thoughts of spring had flooded Barbara's mind since Bobby and Amanda had been returned to her. She felt as though her heart was shooting up a few stalks of grass just like the ground in Dry Creek was. The ground had been frozen all winter, but now, when the sun was shining, it sent up a couple of stalks to see if the season was really changing.

Barbara knew that, for her, one of those stalks was her hope that maybe she'd been wrong about God. She'd seen the concrete love and concern of the people in the church here and she couldn't help but wonder if what they believed was true. How else could these people care so much about each other?

Barbara looked at the clock. Mrs. Hargrove had invited Bobby and Amanda to spend the night at her house so Barbara had the rare luxury of getting dressed without needing to worry about the children. She still had twenty minutes before Carl was due to pick her up for dinner.

Maybe she needed to do something different with her hair, she thought as she stood up. Earlier she'd thought that she should just leave it down. But maybe it would be better to put it up in a twist. And she needed to change her earrings, too. She'd gone from silver dangles to gold posts.

By the time she heard a knock at the outer door, Barbara was wearing black bead earrings and her hair was pulled back with a black clip.

The sheriff noticed right away that Barbara had done something different with her hair. "It looks sophisticated."

Barbara smiled. "Thanks."

The sheriff fretted all the time he and Barbara walked over to the restaurant. He should have worn the suit. Barbara looked too well-dressed for his denim. Women were sensitive to things like that. If he wasn't so worried about his clothes, he would have noticed the activity in the café sooner.

"Oh," Barbara said when the sheriff opened the door to the café for her.

The sheriff grimaced. He hadn't exactly expected the solitude they'd been granted on their last date, but he hadn't expected a convention either. It felt as though every person in Dry Creek was eating in the café tonight.

"It's busy," Barbara said.

The sheriff nodded. Neither one of them had even stepped inside the café yet. "I suppose we should close the door."

The conversation from the tables was a loud rumble. Linda was writing on a small tablet as someone called out an order for chili fries.

"Come on in," the pastor called out from the table where he sat with his wife, Glory, and their twin boys. They were all eating platters of hamburgers and fries.

Once the pastor had greeted the two newcomers, no one else bothered.

The sheriff and Barbara stepped inside and closed the door.

"Is the café running a special?" Barbara asked.

"They always have a Saturday-night special," the sheriff muttered. "I thought it was to encourage couples to date a little."

One of the pastor's twins threw a plastic catsup bottle to a boy at the next table. Somebody somewhere turned up the music. It was a children's song.

"Maybe it's family night," Barbara said.

The sheriff looked around. There wasn't even a free table for them to sit at. He felt like a fool carrying this rose in his hand. Were people so blind they didn't see that here was a couple on a date?

"You're welcome to sit here," Jacob called out from one side of the room. "I can fit you in."

Jacob was sitting at a small table like the one the sheriff and Barbara had had the last time they'd had dinner here.

"Thanks, but we'll wait for a table," the sheriff said. The sheriff decided maybe people hadn't seen the rose. He held it up a little higher. He figured he could live with the teasing he'd take tomorrow morning in church if it would get him a little privacy tonight.

"Suit yourself," Jacob said. He didn't even look at the rose. "But there's plenty of room."

"You're welcome over here," Pete Denning called from his table.

The sheriff couldn't help but notice that Pete had a big table all to himself right next to the kitchen. It looked as if Linda had draped her apron over the other chair at the table.

"Ah, come on." Pete waved them over. "I've got an idea for that campaign slogan you've been working on."

"We have a slogan already," Barbara said.

"We do?" the sheriff whispered. They hadn't worked on the campaign any more. He thought maybe Barbara had forgotten about it. He knew he had.

"Yes," Barbara nodded. "It's Vote for Carl Wall for Sheriff." She turned to the sheriff. "We'll put *Carl Wall* in big letters. These people need to learn your name and start using it."

The sheriff grinned. He couldn't argue with that.

The sheriff figured no one was ever going to notice the rose he held.

"It's a nice night," the sheriff whispered to Barbara. "And there are stars out. We could just get some hamburgers to go and sit outside."

Barbara nodded. "At least it will be quiet enough to talk."

Barbara couldn't help but notice that even though she'd said she wanted it to be quiet enough for talking, she couldn't think of anything to say once she and Carl were outside with their bag of burgers and fries. They were sitting at the top of the church steps and there was quiet all around them. The church had a small light outside its double doors, and someone had turned it on tonight. The light was small enough that they could still look up and see the stars.

Carl had brought a rug out of his trunk that he said he used if he needed to slide under someone's car to repair it.

"It's clean," he assured her as he spread it on the landing at the top of the steps. "I have another one I use if the job is going to involve grease."

Barbara nodded. "You're too kind."

Carl had asked for an extra plastic cup and he'd set the rose up in the center of a napkin that he'd spread for them like a table-cloth. The rose was the perfect touch. Barbara wondered what he had in the envelope he carried.

They ate in silence.

"The hamburgers are good," Barbara finally said.

"It's the cheese," Carl agreed.

There was more silence.

"I haven't thanked you yet for dinner," Barbara said. "It's delicious."

"You don't need to thank me," Carl said with a grimace. "I wanted to talk to you."

"About the campaign?"

"No." Carl frowned. "Actually, the only reason I agreed to a campaign anyway was to spend time with you."

"Oh."

Carl nodded. "I would have campaigned for my competition if I had to in order to spend time with you."

"Oh."

"Of course, I don't have any competition."

Carl was quiet for a moment. "In the campaign, that is."

"Well, it's a good thing," Barbara said with a smile. "You'd lose for sure if people saw you campaigning for someone else."

"You're not upset?"

"No, I think I'm flattered."

Carl was quiet for another minute. "There are some things about me you don't know."

"Do you want to tell me?"

Carl nodded. "I was raised in foster homes. A whole bunch of them. One after another. I don't think I'm very good at family stuff. Don't know how it's done."

Barbara smiled. "There are days when I'm not sure I know either. But, if you're asking my opinion, I have to say that you've been wonderful with both Amanda and Bobby. Bobby practically idolizes you."

"He's grateful," Carl said. "He was scared, and I'm the one who got him out of it."

Barbara shrugged. "That's most of what parenting is."

Carl was silent for a moment as he took another bite of his hamburger. "Have you heard any more about old man Gossett renting you his place?"

"Mrs. Hargrove says his nephew is real sick, and Mr. Gossett is thinking the nephew and his family might want to move here. Good air for the children and all that."

"I'm sorry it's not for rent."

Barbara nodded. "I expect they'll wonder why that fence is painted so nice and white when the house is all weathered."

Carl grunted. "Never heard of anyone complaining about a free paint job."

Barbara sighed. "I think it was the fence I liked so much about the place."

"I have a fence." Carl's face paled. "I mean, I don't have a house like you'd want, but I have a fence."

Barbara got very still.

Carl was silent for a minute. "I told you I wasn't very good at this kind of thing. I had it all thought out in my mind, and now I got ahead of myself with the fence so I may as well just spit it out."

Carl swallowed hard. "I live in a trailer, so it's nothing fancy. It suits me fine, but I know it's no house. The thing is, though, that I've got plans all drawn up for a log house that could be built on my place. I brought the plans to show you later. The house would be right back in the trees and it'd be no trouble at all to put a fence around it. I know you're real set on a good house."

"I—" Barbara started.

Carl took a quick breath and kept going. "Let me finish. I know you don't see us as being anything more than friends. But things can change."

"I—" Barbara began again.

"I'm not asking anything right now, so if that's what you're thinking, you can rest easy," Carl said. "I figure you need a full year of grieving before you're over your ex-husband, and I got time to wait."

"I—" Barbara began again and was surprised when he let her keep talking. "Well, I—let me see. First, I know that a house is just a house. It is the people who make the home. Second, yes, things can change. And, third, I'm grieving for my lost dreams, but not my ex-husband. The man doesn't even care about our children."

"So things can change?" the sheriff asked.

Barbara couldn't help but notice that the sheriff's face wasn't pale anymore. In fact, it was looking, well, certainly more healthy than before. "Slowly, things can change slowly."

"We've got time," Carl said. His face was beaming now. "I figure we're due to drive into Miles City for dinner next time."

"And miss out on this?"

Carl slid a little closer to her. "Well, we can see the stars from here."

Barbara slid a little closer to him as well. She remembered that there was more than one way to see stars when Carl was around.

Maybe things wouldn't need to go all that slowly, she thought, as Carl bent to kiss her. No, she thought, they might not need to go slowly at all.

Epilogue

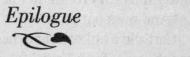

The wedding was to be in the fall. Barbara and Carl had both gone through premarital counseling with the pastor of the Dry Creek Church and decided to add a confession of faith to their wedding vows.

They were working on the wording of their confession of faith with Mrs. Hargrove and her Sunday-school class. The children were excited that they could play a part and, under Mrs. Hargrove's guidance, were coming up with some good suggestions. The children's favorite suggestion was to work in the story of Daniel in the lion's den.

"You could say that you realize it is important to trust God when the beasts of life are coming at you," Mrs. Hargrove suggested.

"Lions—they need to say lions," Bobby said. "When the lions are coming at them."

Barbara and Carl were regular helpers in Mrs. Hargrove's class now, so they were there for the discussion.

"We could say lions," Carl said.

It was going to be a unique wedding anyway. The bride had decided she wanted to pour the coffee for her reception. She'd ordered a cream-colored gown that was frothy with lace and had the added value of having a veil that was short enough so that it wouldn't get in the way when she poured that coffee.

The bride was debating sending into Billings for a rental silver urn for the coffee just so the ceremony would have a little extra polish.

Then, a few weeks before the wedding, the bride noticed that a shy young woman had just moved into town. The woman sat in the back pew of the Dry Creek Church and never stayed long to talk with anyone. The Sunday before the wedding, the bride asked the woman if she'd be willing to pour coffee for her wedding reception.

"You don't know what this means to me," the young woman said. She was wearing a modest cotton dress that had seen many washings. Her shoes were a little scuffed, as if they had been polished and repolished until the leather refused to take any more black polish.

The bride just smiled. "I'm glad you will enjoy it. Welcome to Dry Creek."

The groom was holding the bride's hand and, when the young woman left, he whispered to his wife-to-be. "That was generous of you."

The bride had told him about the coffee. "Mrs. Hargrove already asked me to pour coffee on election day."

"Won't that prejudice people to vote for me?"

The bride grinned. "I hope so. We never did get around to making that sign."

"Who needs a sign when I have you?" the sheriff said as he bent down to give the bride a quick kiss.

There were half a dozen people still in the church and no one even looked up at the kiss. The sight of Carl kissing Barbara didn't even make a good story any longer. It happened all the time.

* * * * *

Dear Reader,

I wish for all of you many days of pouring coffee and sharing fellowship at your church. Our lives are meant to be lived in community and, as often as not, that means taking time to serve each other.

I thoroughly enjoy writing about the church in Dry Creek, primarily because it is a focal point of the community. It is the place where troubles and joys are shared with the whole town.

I'd like to give a nod of thanks to people like Mrs. Hargrove who help such local communities run. I've known many women—and men—like her in the churches I have attended. You'll usually find such people in the kitchens or in the Sunday school rooms or serving communion on certain Sundays. Without them, our shared communities wouldn't be nearly as rich as they are.

Sincerely,

Janet Tronstad

QUESTIONS FOR DISCUSSION

1. Barbara was reluctant to get married again because Neal had not been faithful to her when they were married. Do you think there is anything she could have done to save her marriage to Neal early on?

2. Even though Barbara was not a Christian when she was married to Neal, she was deeply disappointed when he was unfaithful. She had married Neal thinking their life would be a good one together. We all have times when things do not turn out as we thought they would. What are some of those things in your life (past or present)? What did God do to intervene in the situation (or has He)?

3. The people in the Dry Creek church clearly pray for each other. Do you have people in your life who pray for you? Do you pray for others? How does it make you feel to have people praying for you?

4. How do you decide who to pray for in your own prayer time? Do you ever add someone who is a newcomer to your community or church?

5. As you read the book, you probably identified with Barbara's desire to belong to the community of Dry Creek. Think of a community or group where you feel you belong. What actions/people give you that feeling?

6. God calls all His children to belong to the community of Christians. In what ways does this happen? Is there a difference between the way we belong to a church and the way we belong to other organizations?

7. Barbara believed that the people of Dry Creek were watching her before they decided to let her into their community. Do you believe we should watch people before we fully accept them into our community? (Think of your community where you live and then also of your church community.)

8. In what concrete ways could your church community be more welcoming to newcomers?

Turn the page for a preview of
THE SISTERHOOD
OF THE DROPPED STITCHES,
the first book in a new Love Inspired series
from Janet Tronstad,
available in February 2007.

I wish I could say we all agreed to call ourselves The Sisterhood of the Dropped Stitches that first night, but that wouldn't be true. I've been voted to be the one to tell you how we started six years ago, and I have everyone's permission to tell you how it was with us back then. We were just getting to know each other and we couldn't agree on anything.

Lizabett voted for The Sisterhood because she thought we were serious about knitting and should have a name with "Stitches" in it. She liked things to be clear and identifiable.

As for me, I was so distraught that I didn't care what we called ourselves, although I do remember thinking there was some kind of cosmic justice in calling ourselves the Dropped Stitches. I mean, if you looked at our lives, you could see we were like dropped stitches.

I used to wonder if God had been watching some landmark game on television when He made us and that's why He missed the stitches that ended up letting us get cancer. Breast cancer. Bone cancer. Lymphoma. We had the full range. I didn't mind telling Him it was a pretty big miss when He dropped the stitches on us. The stitch He missed in me changed my life.

There is nothing like a diagnosis of breast cancer to scare away a girl's future. I dropped out of my UCLA classes to cope with the chemo and decided to say no to dates.

The resentment about how unfair my life had become festered in me, but it wasn't something I could talk to my doctors about, especially not when they were busy trying to save my life. It seemed I should at least be able to handle my feelings. I mean, they were only feelings—they weren't tumors. All I needed was someone to talk to about things, preferably someone who was a professional and would know what to say.

Rose was a student counselor at the hospital. She was the one who first decided the four of us—me (I'm Marilee), Carly, Becca, and Lizabett—needed to be in a group together. She said we should be like normal teenagers and have a club.

I remember wondering at the time just how normal she expected us to be when we were all staring death in the face. Rose had been an elementary school teacher for some years before she went back to graduate school, so she was prepared for life. Still, she looked as scared as I felt.

I suspected it was worse for Rose to comfort me than her usual clients because she and I had become close in the weeks I'd known her. I had to become close to her. She was my rock. I talked to her about the things I couldn't talk to my mom or dad about. I needed her. That didn't stop me from telling her I didn't want to belong to any stupid cancer group though.

"Cancer? Who said anything about a cancer group?" Rose said after a brief pause. "No, no, I'm talking about starting a knitting group. Lots of people knit these days."

I know the knitting idea just flew into Rose's head when I was being so stubborn about joining a cancer group. But once she said it, the whole thing seemed to take root. Apparently, her farm-raised grandmother had taught Rose how to knit and she was happy—maybe even relieved—to teach us. She told me later she was glad she could do something concrete with her hands to help us.

Rose's grandmother was also fond of old sayings and quotes, so Rose decided one of us would bring an inspirational quote to each meeting in case we ran out of things to talk about while we sat there tangled in all our yarn.

I had been telling my troubles to Rose when she thought of having a club. I'm not sure how I would have gotten through all the chemo and the scared feelings without The Sisterhood. Before long, I would have knitted those scarves with my teeth if I'd had to just so I could keep meeting with them.

This was almost six years ago and we all made it.

Let me repeat that. *We all made it.* Three cheers. I still feel good every time I say that.

We all passed our cancer-free dates last year and officially became Survivors. There hasn't been a week in all that time when we've considered stopping The Sisterhood for more than a holiday break. If it's not Thanksgiving or Christmas, every Thursday the five of us meet in The Pews—that's the name of my uncle Lou's diner. We sit at the big table in the back room and knit.

These days, one of my favorite times is when someone brings a quote to the meeting. I think it was the quotes that made us turn so reflective that we decided to set some goals last year. Reaching the five-year mark for each of us was such a major thing. I can't describe it. We couldn't think of anything big enough to celebrate so Rose suggested we all make a special goal for the next year—something that would show we were taking our lives back.

All I can say about those goals is that I wish I'd listened to my inner cynic. My cynic knows this female-male attraction can't be goaled into being. Finding the right guy to date—someone who really curls your toes, as Rose would say—should never be part of anyone's must-meet annual goals. Love doesn't work on a schedule.

Trust me on this. Let me tell you how Becca set her goal. She has always wanted to become a lawyer. She was already taking some pre-law classes, so she set her goal as being chosen to be an intern with a local judge for next summer. The judge always selects two pre-law students to work with her from June to September. It's apparently a big deal because the judge is one of the best according to Becca, who knows these kinds of things. Getting that internship is a nice, sensible goal and, if I weren't so happy in my job, I would have chosen one to advance my career as well.

Not that all of our goals were about jobs.

Carly decided to get a Maine coon cat. She'd always wanted a cat, she told us, but she couldn't get one because she is allergic to them. The Maine coon cat, however, is a purebred that has different dander from other cats or something. Anyway, it has long hair just like Carly likes, but it is still okay for people with allergies.

At first, I was skeptical. I couldn't imagine Carly having any animal with coon in its name. I mean, she is just so classy. But then Carly told us that this particular breed of cat is descended from six house cats that Marie

Antoinette sent to Wiscassett, Maine, when she was hoping to escape from France during the French Revolution. The cats were to be there to welcome her when she made it to the New World. That sounded more like Carly. She liked movie stars and royalty. She'd love having a cat whose ancestors belonged to Marie Antoinette.

Of course, the cat was not cheap. It cost two thousand dollars and it took Carly months to find one. In fact, she just got her cat a week or so ago.

I was happy when she met her goal. I even sent her home with some raw steak from the diner after our meeting last week.

Lizabett always surprised us by saying she'd always wanted to perform in a ballet, twirling and dipping around on stage in a costume. Her eyes lit up just talking about it. So, of course, that had to be her goal. She signed up for classes before the month was out at a community dance studio over in La Cañada, and is performing this coming Sunday in a production of *Swan Lake*. She showed us a picture of her costume last week. It's all white net and froth. She'll look adorable on stage. And the performance will be just in time for her to meet her goal.

Thursday—one week from today—is the date when the goals are due to be completed, and I'm the only one who hasn't done what I'd said I would do. You would think I'd get some extra credit for writing up this description of how we started The Sisterhood, but no one seems willing to let me slide on my goal. And I'm not even close to meeting it.

My goal is to have three dates with a man (or men) I could see myself with long-term. Carly suggested the long-term addition, and I know now I shouldn't have agreed to it. Carly has so many offers she can afford to be picky about things like long-term attraction.

I'm not Carly. If men ask me out, it is obviously because they like me. I'm certainly not Rose Queen material like Carly is. I need to count all my dates, long-term and short-term.

Even at that, I wasn't worried when I made the goal because one year is a long time. How could I have known I'd procrastinate? The problem was I didn't want to be on a manhunt. I just wanted it to happen, you know?

I think it was all the philosophizing with

the quotes that wore down my good sense to the point that I even made this kind of a goal. The others brought in ones that made a person think anything was possible if the whole group worked on it. After we'd been bald and scared together, we didn't have any barriers left. Once we'd reached our five-year marker, anything seemed possible.

Usually, that kind of soaring enthusiasm is a good thing, but lately—well, at least since next Thursday is coming up so fast—I've begun to wonder if some of those in The Sisterhood haven't grown *too* supportive of seeing me meet my goal. They keep saying Friday, Saturday and Sunday are all excellent date nights. I'll be doing good if they don't hurry me out of our meeting tonight with orders to find some man on the street to have coffee with before the diner closes.

Come to think of it, there is that coffee place in De Lacy alley. There might be a busboy there willing to sit down and have a cup of coffee with me. I wonder if that would count?

2 Love Inspired novels and 2 mystery gifts... Absolutely FREE!

Visit
www.LoveInspiredBooks.com
for your two FREE books, sent directly to you!

BONUS: Choose between regular print or our NEW larger print format!

There's no catch! You're under no obligation to buy anything. We charge nothing—ZERO—for your first shipment. And you don't have to make any minimum number of purchases.

You'll like the convenience of home delivery at our special discount prices, and you'll love your free subscription to Steeple Hill News, our members-only newsletter.

We hope that after receiving your free books, you'll want to remain a subscriber. But the choice is yours—to continue or cancel, anytime at all! So why not take us up on our invitation, with no risk of any kind!

Love Inspired

LIGEN06